BLESSED BY A SAINT

STORIES ABOUT GRACE

BY GERALD L. BOWEN JR.

DORRANCE
PUBLISHING CO
EST. 1920
PITTSBURGH, PENNSYLVANIA 15222

Dorrance Publishing Co
701 Smithfield Street
Pittsburgh, PA 15222
Visit our website at *www.dorrancebookstore.com*

ISBN: 978-1-4809-1173-4
eISBN 978-1-4809-1495-7

BLESSED BY A SAINT

This is a collection of inspirational short stories about a little girl with special needs. The stories are fiction, but are based on actual events. The net proceeds received from the sale of this book will be donated to charities for the disabled.

"The quality of society is measured by the respect it shows towards the weakest of its members."

Saint John Paul II

A Few Facts about Saint John Paul II

He was born Karol Wojtyla on May 18, 1920, in the Polish village of Wadowice, a gift from God to devout Catholic parents. His father was a military man for the Polish Army and his mother a convent-educated homemaker. By the age of twenty-one, he had lost his mother, his only brother, and his father due to illnesses and was therefore essentially orphaned. From an early age, Karol displayed intellectual gifts, a love of sports, and a gentle, pious nature. He had a passion for the theatre, literature, and the game of soccer. He also enjoyed skiing, hiking, and the outdoors. As a young man, he worked in a quarry and a chemical plant. He somehow managed to survive the brutal German occupation of Poland during the late 1930s and during World War II, including the infamous Black Sunday on August 6, 1944, where the German Army marched up and down the town streets, hauling in thousands of boys and young men to quell an alleged uprising.

In 1946, after four years in the seminary, he was ordained and became Father Wojtyla. As a priest, he was a charismatic teacher, philosopher, and leader for his congregations and quickly rose within the ranks of the Church in Poland. In 1954, he also became a teacher at the Catholic University of Lublin. He was a significant contributor in the sessions at the Second Vatican Council (Vatican II) during the mid-1960s. He became a Cardinal in 1967. During the Cold War years, Cardinal Wojtyla was a beacon of hope and a source of strength for the Polish people against the Communists. In 1978, he was elected by the College of Cardinals in Rome and became the first Polish pope in history. He took the name Pope John Paul II. During his papacy, he traveled the world like none before him and he spread Christianity in the east, the west, and in third-world countries. Everywhere he went he proclaimed the word of the Gospel and professed the virtues of peace and love over war. He suffered an assassination attempt in 1982, and in the ultimate act of reconciliation, he later forgave the man who shot him.

As Pope, he had the insight and initiative to reach out to the younger generations and with them started World Youth Day. He met with presidents, kings, queens, world leaders, and famous celebrities during his twenty-seven-year reign, which was the third-longest papal reign in the Church's history. He utilized his relationships with powerful people he knew to effectuate social change throughout the world. In his declining years, he became a victim of various debilitating ailments, which virtually disabled him physically, yet he still managed to rule the Church with his mind and his strong will. He fought tirelessly for the sanctity of life and constantly reminded the world of the responsibility for society to help the less fortunate of God's people. He was one of the biggest and most effective advocates for the disabled in the history of the world.

In 2005, he died after a lengthy illness but while showing the world that there was a dignity to the death process as well. On April 27, 2014, Pope John Paul II was canonized in Rome, Italy, after the shortest waiting period in the history of the modern Catholic Church.

CONTENTS

 *A collection of comments about Grace from family, friends, and those she inspires.

Foreword

As a devout Catholic, I considered it both a privilege and a responsibility when asked to write the foreword for this unique book. This collection of sixteen short stories about a severely physically and mentally disabled child named Grace, who inspires the world around her, is not only a provocative and entertaining piece of literature, but the book is certainly much more than that. This book promotes the principles of unconditional love, perseverance, and the acceptance of God's plan for all of us in life. The book also intuitively asks society as a whole to have a greater understanding and appreciation for individuals with special needs. This book is a rare example in today's materialistic world, of an author whose primary motivation, for once, is not about making money, but rather to inspire and to help as many people as possible.

Throughout the book, the message is resoundingly clear about the firm belief shared by many that little Grace Bowen may very well be an angel sent from God and doing his work here on earth. The story "Angels on Earth," in fact, promotes the concept that perhaps all severe mentally handicapped individuals (those that have never sinned) are God's army of angels in this world. Overall, the different stories, using different methods, reveal the details of a magical occurrence in Rome, Italy, back in the Millennium Jubilee year in the Catholic Church and how that single poignant against-all-the-odds moment has had an incredible ripple effect for little Grace, her family, and those around them. The sixteen stories were originally written to each stand alone in the various short story genres, but the concept of the book came into fruition to celebrate the magnificent and deserved event of Pope John Paul II becoming a saint. The picture on the front cover provides a powerful platform for the written pages that follow.

The book, first and foremost, tells the reader about the trials and tribulations, along with the harsh realities often involved with raising a severely handicapped child. The author describes the incredible suffering and intense medical care that little Grace has gone through in her life so far and still goes through every day. However, the author weaves this information in compelling stories about love, joy, perseverance, acceptance, and family. Rather than trying to evoke sympathy because of Grace's unfortunate disabilities, the stories are insightful, have humor, and promote character strength rising from adversity. The stories "True Communion" and "Life Is a Picnic," for example, each tell a tale that gives the reader a charming message about doing our best with what we are given in life and challenges each individual to appreciate those around us.

Three of the stories are the foundation for the book. The story "Defining Grace" reveals the different definitions of the fascinating word that is not only the name of a girl, but also carries with it so many other significant meanings. The story "Touched by Grace" is written using vignettes and tells the reader the captivating separate stories of sixteen special rosaries, which found their way into the lives of individuals. Each of the vignettes is a touching account and powerful example of how people's lives can be greatly affected by God and the simple effort of others. And, the story "Knowing Grace" is intended to be a glimpse for the reader into the everyday world of a family with a severely handicapped child, while also discovering the magic of the book's main character.

Several of the stories are written from the fascinating perspective of Grace herself—looking at life through her eyes, which is truly thought-provoking and emotionally powerful, especially since it is clear that due to her severe mental handicaps, we cannot know for sure what she is thinking. The story "The Best Gift I Could Think Of" is a beautiful presentation of a daughter's love for her mother using the setting of a Christmas Eve. The story "Easter at Gamma's," meanwhile, is a charming tale telling the reader some neat historical and religious facts about the holiday of Easter, all weaved into a weekend visit to Grace's beloved grandmother's house. "A Christmas Concert" is another holiday celebration of family and music from Grace's point of view. In addition, the story "A Special Bedtime Prayer" gives the reader a visit into little Grace's possible prayerful thoughts as she drifts off to sleep one particular evening.

Many of the stories are written with the dual purpose of celebrating all the different worlds that Grace encounters in her life and illustrating her effect on people, while also meant to appreciate the many loving and caring individuals that have come to know her. An underlying premise throughout the entire book is that the fortuitous incidents described that have occurred to Grace in her life are not mere coincidences. Those stories include: "Vision," "The Lov bug," "Amazing Grace Margaret," "The Gala," and "Looking for Grace." The book overall is intended to have universal implications to help people with disabilities all over the world, but one thing is also quite clear—this is a Philadelphia story.

Fittingly, the last story in this collection is entitled, "Talking with Grace," which is a short three-page question and answer session between Grace and her father, but, in fact, could be between Grace and almost anyone. The dialogue with Grace enables the reader to truly appreciate the unique combination of the abilities and disabilities that God gave to Grace. The story tells the reader so much about her simply by utilizing a few basic questions.

The book also contains numerous photographs, which are utterly fascinating by themselves, and independently tell the story of what Grace is all about, what she has gone through in her life, and exudes her spiritual qualities.

The book aptly concludes with comments about Grace from some of those who know her, which the author hopes enables the book's premise to come full circle. I say it does. What better way to conclude a book about the inspirational and spiritual qualities of a special needs child sent from God to make the world a better place, than to read the witness and testimony by those she has inspired. Reading the quotes and comments, I was brought to tears and I am paused to wonder how many others there might be out there to add to the list. Certainly, the world needs more "grace."

Susan Carney Smuck, R.N.

ACKNOWLEDGMENTS

Any acknowledgment for this book must start with recognizing and thanking my wonderful wife, Doreen, for her inspiration, encouragement, and overall patience with this thirteen-year project to write a book about our special needs daughter. My wife listened for countless hours to my story ideas and my rambling book brainstorming, which must have been exhausting for her. More than anything, though, her devotion and love for our handicapped daughter, along with her intense commitment to our entire family, gave me the ability to accomplish this goal.

As some know, the trials, tribulations, and stress of a severely disabled child can be devastating to a family or it can sometimes somehow make the family unit stronger. Because of my wife, we are fortunate to be in the latter group. Despite all the tough times we encountered, we have grown over the years to consider ourselves to be lucky. We truly believe that our daughter Grace is an angel from God and was given to us for a reason.

Now there is a long list of other people I would also like to thank, starting with my assistant, co-writer, computer consultant, social media liaison, and beautiful younger teenage daughter Shannon Bowen, who helped me and inspired me on many occasions and, particularly, over the last year or so with the precise motivating words, "Come on, Dad; get the book done already."

In addition, I want to thank my thoughtful mother-in-law, Margaret Obal, who helped us in every way possible over the years and also gave me the first real push to write the book on our plane ride coming back from Rome in mid-

December of 2000, when she said with a slight tone in her voice, "Well, then, stop talking about it and do it."

In addition, I want to thank all of Grace's doctors and their staffs, all the hospitals, nurses and medical personnel for the incredible medical care Grace has received during her lifetime so far as well as all those who will most certainly be needed in the future.

I'd also like to thank my personal writing muse, Susan Smuck and her husband Bill, who would come to my law office on occasion, read my stories, and then discuss them over a lunch together, thereby providing me with a much-needed sounding board at the beginning of my writing journey. Also, thanks to the Bucks County Writer's Workshop for helping me to understand the tools necessary to put my ideas into action.

Next on the list is our wonderful parish priest Father Joseph McLaughlin, who cares so dearly about helping the disabled and was so proactive to help champion the unique inspirational qualities of our daughter Grace by writing about her all the time through the years in our parish newsletters. In addition, I wish to thank the leadership of the Archdiocese of Philadelphia, who made the trip to Rome possible; Cardinal John Patrick Foley (deceased) for his thoughtfulness over the years; and the many dedicated, loving and hard-working people involved with Catholic Social Services in Philadelphia, especially those who have been directly involved with Grace's care.

I have said many times, that our Grace somehow belongs to everyone she meets. She is truly a messenger of God's love, to be shared in this world.

I'd also like to thank Mr. and Mrs. Gene Wolstenholme for their incredible generosity and help with getting this book published. Their expression of Christian values is nothing short of remarkable. Further, I want to express my gratitude and appreciation to the writing professionals who helped me make it to the finish line with this book. Last but not least, I thank my daughter Grace herself, for all the reasons I hope you will find evident when reading the pages herein.

DEFINING GRACE

*The Bible's Definition: GRACE, STATE OF. The person who is
living in friendship with God. This gift is offered by God to all,
but may be accepted or rejected by each individual.*

I sat there that Sunday morning at the end of the pew, waiting for the Mass
to start. Our four-year-old daughter Shannon was sleeping next to me in her
stroller, which I had placed like an extra chair outside the end of the row.
Shannon's feet were dangling out the front of the much traveled and multi-
purpose vehicle for kids. My wife was seated up closer to the altar with our
older child. Sitting there, I looked all around at the beautiful old church. As
my eyes wandered, I thought back to the darkest day of my life and the multitude of events that had transpired since then. My eyes may be gazing forward
and about, but my reflections led me away. I was brought back to a moment
in time, six years prior.

It was November 1, 1994 – All Saints' Day. A day my wife and I will never
forget. We were a young married couple and it was her first pregnancy. We
had illusions of grandeur.

Amid the tension and confusion of the hospital delivery room that morning, the obstetrician eventually spoke the words that would change our lives
forever. "There is something wrong with the baby," said the doctor. "The head
is much too large for the birth canal." With that blunt statement of fact, our
world altered drastically and many things started to happen quickly. The hospital's high-risk, maternity team was alerted, consulted, and eventually took

over the delivery procedure. STAT Level-II ultrasounds were ordered. The problems, we soon learned, were numerous and major.

The level II, more sophisticated ultrasounds, showed that our baby had grossly enlarged ventricles in her head. The condition was known in medical circles as hydrocephalus, which means water on the brain. As a result, the baby's head was huge—forty-four centimeters in diameter, much larger than normal. We were told that the chances of the baby making it out the birth canal alive were slim. And, if the baby did make it through the birth, the child, we were abruptly advised, would most likely be severely impaired. It was all quite a shock to say the least. The orbit of our world had changed dramatically since we left our house only a few hours earlier that morning.

All our pre-conceived notions and elaborate expectations dissipated. The expected wonders of birth and the projected excitement of the moment were now replaced with a paralyzing fear of the unknown and a struggle for life itself—both for the baby and for my wife. To attribute a well-known phrase… "This definitely wasn't what the doctor had ordered."

My bride labored intensely that seemingly endless afternoon, pushing for hours without any kind of break. The ice chip theory we had practiced in our Lamaze class became like first grade reading material. The delivery turned into a prolonged surgical operation. Entire medical shifts came and went. After a while, I didn't recognize anyone in the room except for my wife and me. The baby's head was swollen badly and now stuck in the birth canal. The options for a C-Section had been dismissed because of surrounding complications and risks for my wife's health. I stood there helpless, cringing as my wife suffered. She was in excruciating pain as the doctors used special maternity clamps to try and pull the baby out. Worse than the pain, my wife was scared. The face of a woman fighting with all her energy to bring a sick child into the world is a sad state of affairs; an extended battle is cruel. Plus, no one even asked me if I wanted to cut the cord.

At exactly 5:04 that evening, our first child entered the world. It was a girl. The baby weighed six pounds, thirteen ounces, and was nineteen and three-quarters inches long. Her head was grossly misshapen—much larger than normal and vastly disproportionate to the rest of the tiny body. The forehead frontal lobes protruded badly. The bone plates, present at the top of a person's skull, were completely unattached and out of place.

I was afraid to hold my own child. As the nurses took the baby to the incubator, I bit my lip to wake myself—trying to somehow stop the carousel. Our precious little daughter looked like an alien. It was an expectant parent's worst nightmare.

My unpleasant recollections of the delivery of our first child were suddenly interrupted as someone tapped on my shoulder from the pew behind me. I came out of my dazed trance and looked around. It was a man about 25 years of age. He was a Caucasian gentleman, about medium build, and he had thick black hair with a few premature streaks of gray. It was apparent to me right away that the man had Down's syndrome. I turned around completely to see what he wanted. He was talking fast and I couldn't quite understand what he was trying to say. I greeted him cordially in a patient, interested voice, which is a trained and learned response. He was either asking a question or making a statement. His comments though were not directed at me. He was merely excited. He kept tapping me on the shoulder repeatedly. Trying to be considerate, I smiled back at him and then politely nodded my head in a confirming fashion. Most people in today's day and age would have perhaps, been annoyed; however, life's experiences truly change one's viewpoints. He was only being friendly. He was just a little different.

⤳⤳

As I turned back around in my seat, my thoughts returned to the traumatic hospital events during that difficult day in 1994. I recalled being in the pediatric neurologist's office shortly after the delivery and listening to words that sounded like Greek. Now, as a lawyer, I'd always felt I knew more medical terms than most, but this was humbling. Nothing fully prepares you for the curveballs of life.

The neurologist explained that, "Lightning strikes, accidents happen, and things can go wrong with the course of nature." He told me, "No one was at fault, no one was to blame—sometimes, there's no certain cause for a developmental brain anomaly."

I remember clenching my fists and saying to myself, bitterly underneath my breath, *most of the time people don't know what the hell that means*. A developmental brain anomaly or a congenital malformation, I quickly learned, is the medical jargon for things that can happen and the doctors don't even know why. All things said, the doctor's words were not really helpful and far from comforting.

Several medical consultations later, the diagnosis for our infant daughter was confirmed. The unfavorable findings were: severe maximal hydrocephalus;

indications consistent with lobar holoprosencephaly; a dysmorphic brain; caudal regression syndrome; cortical blindness; nystagmus; amblyopia; Arnold Chiari I syndrome; a neurogenic bladder; neurogenic bowels; microcephalus (meaning a very small brain); hyperopia; and estropia. The other broader explanation is a neurologic problem with the midline of the brain that caused all kinds of things to simply go haywire. My personal choice for explaining to the well-wishers and nosey-bodies who insisted on details in the ensuing weeks after the birth, was to state that while the baby was in the uterus, a kind of aneurysm occurred in the baby's head causing a blockage, which then prevented the normal growth of the brain and, therefore, many other problems to occur. No positive spin was available.

The next course of action during the days after the birth was, by all accounts and in one form or another, a ventricular shunt procedure. The necessary shunt procedure involved making an incision in the baby's head and another in the stomach, so that the doctors could insert a long thin tube to run inside the body. The tube would drain the excessive spinal fluid from the head down into the abdominal cavity for absorption. We needed to take the extra fluid off the brain as soon as possible, too, or else our daughter could die because of the cranial pressure being exerted on the spinal column. We were on a whirlwind of a ride and traveling no place pleasant.

∽∾∾

My thoughts of the past were interrupted again and I slowly returned consciously to the Mass, which I could see was now just about to start. According to rumors swirling amongst the crowd around me, the big doors in the back of the church were about to open any minute. I looked down and saw that my daughter Shannon was still fast asleep. Thank God for that. It was always tough with young ones in church.

My eyes then began to roam the vast surroundings again and observe the people around me. I took off my suit jacket and put it on Shannon for use as a blanket. It didn't matter, though, she would probably just kick it off. That's why we nicknamed her "The Squirmer." Whenever she would jump up into bed with us to sleep at night, she wiggled and flailed all over the bed, sending the covers every which way. She was the only one who ever got any sleep and she was completely oblivious to the disruption she caused. The very notion of sleep prompted me to yawn and I quickly raised my hand to cover my mouth. I hadn't slept much the night before and my eyelids grew heavy.

A few days after the birth, the city's best pediatric neurosurgeon described to us the pros, cons, risks, possibilities, and realities of the ventricular shunt procedure. Optimism filled the room like a hot air balloon on a clear summer day. "Sometimes," she said, "the brain can act like a sponge. Once the spinal fluid is drained from the ventricles, the pressure is lessened and the brain has the opportunity to rebound. The brain mass could then expand its shape—maybe, if we're really lucky, back to the normal size. Talking best case scenario, the developmental impairments may not be catastrophic. We put the shunt in and drain the spinal fluid out of the ventricles. After that, we wait and see—we wait about six months or so."

Well, the shunt procedure was technically a surgical success; however, over the next few months, we became very aware that the best case scenario had not occurred—not even close. Unfortunately, the brain did not rebound like a sponge.

Succinctly, the prognosis overall was poor. Our little girl, our little angel, would most likely have the cognitive abilities of a baby for the rest of her life. She would need constant medical attention and she would require all kinds of different therapies; with little hope, we were told, for any meaningful progress. We were also advised that she would probably never walk and she would likely be blind. The odds of her even crawling were slim. Certainly, she would never be able to care for herself. For some odd reason, I kept wondering if this also meant that she would never be able to ride a bicycle. In precise technical terms, she was considered profoundly retarded.

∽∾∽

As I opened my eyes and repositioned myself in the pew to get more comfortable, my attention focused on the present-day happenings. I began to take notice of the spectacular interior features of the great church all around me. I found myself staring in wonderment at the tall, sculpted pillars that stood approximately eighty feet high throughout the church. The enormous pillars led your eyes up to a series of circular painted portraits, each with gold trim, placed high on the walls and all running horizontally down the aisles. The gold-embroidered portraits depicted all the popes in the rich history of the Roman Catholic Church going back to Saint Peter. High above the splendid old paintings were magnificent stained-glass windows, which both captivated and fascinated the eye. On this beautiful morning, the sun beamed brilliantly through the stained-glass windows, like water cascading over a scenic mountain waterfall.

The altar was located up at the front of the church—a most majestic sight and surrounded by pews on all sides. According to our Mass booklets, the altar had been constructed over a thousand years before, in the time of the early Christians. The altar was made of white Italian marble with a mahogany arch overhead and was elevated several steps above ground level. From a distance, the altar appeared as if it were its own building-within-a-building, like a magnificent steeple, which was taken from a roof and brought inside.

The imposing four-foot high candles on top of the altar also impressed me and reminded me subconsciously of being enlightened by so many over the last six years. For example, someone a long time ago had extended the wonderful old saying that "God only gives to us what we can handle." Another literary genius had authored the classic adage that, "Everything happens for a reason." Well, both individuals, I would bet, were never the parents of a severely handicapped child; and please tell me who espoused these timeless phrases, so I can go have a long, rough debate with them on the issues. For them, to them, I would profess in reply with my own adage, "The roads of life are learned once traveled and not before. Anyone can merely have directions."

In truth, people in our situation typically first ask, "Why me?" They want to know why it happened to them. Some never get past that stark psychological reality. Many, however, graduate into anger—hating God, hating each other, and resenting people with healthy children. The phase after anger is usually about assessing fault, but most couples don't get that far. From the very beginning, we had been advised by the hospital social workers that approximately eighty-five percent of couples with severely handicapped children end up in divorce for various reasons—quite disturbing odds.

In the fault analysis, the doctors, naturally, are the initial targets. After the examination of the doctors, you look oddly at each other for a long while. Perceptions of blame can be directed in many forms and fashions. Tough questions get asked and family histories are explored. Nasty implications and inferences are offered by insensitive or unknowing family members. Often in the end, no answers are found. At some point, depression usually sets in and that stage has real staying power. Feeling sorry for oneself never seems to go out of style. Meanwhile, you are so stressed out and overwhelmed with the everyday tasks of caring for a very involved, chronically-ill, severely-disabled child that heads are spinning. Sometimes, life simply gets a whole lot harder.

～∽～

There was one positive item for my wife and I that stood out during those difficult early years. Our baby, our sick little daughter, looked like an angel. She
had curly golden blond hair in swirling locks about her head. She had sky blue
eyes, which, to our dismay, were often crossed or turned out toward the sides;
the paradox of beautiful eyes on a child who could not see. Her face was like
that of a porcelain china doll with cheeks red and rosy. When she was asleep,
all seemed at peace with the world and as if nothing was wrong with her. She
had the smallest little button nose, thin red lips, and a subtle, tiny chin. She
had bird-like hands with slender fingers. Her long, black eyelashes fluttered
like butterfly kisses—the lashes seeming too big for her face. We constantly
found ourselves amazed with her beauty, while at the same time, totally distraught with her exasperating medical conditions.

～∽～

Just then, I stood up along with everyone around me and I observed as the imposing forty-foot wooden doors at the back of the great church started to open
and I heard the music which began to play. The impressive, sixty-member
choir, assembled around the altar, led the faithful in singing the entrance hymn.
People in the crowd started to cry at the mere sight of the opening doors alone.
The basilica was now filled to capacity with 13,000 people—either the handicapped, their family members, or those that cared for them. The crosses of
life and the pains of the journey were visible on their faces. Those that could
rose to their feet. Many of the women in the crowd waved their special Jubilee
scarves in anticipation. It was clear to me that a group of this nature did not
want for motivation. This was their Super Bowl and "it" was happening.

First, a parade of priests entered the church and proceeded down the main
aisle with all the proper pomp and circumstance befitting a king. In the waves
of the loyal religious foot soldiers, I saw our own parish pastor who had joined
our group on our pilgrimage. He had flown over separately on his own. He
was walking in the procession beside a priest-friend of his from the country of
India. Next, I observed a litany of the most powerful of Rome—Cardinals,
Bishops, as they all made their way into the church. And, at the back of the
great procession was His Holiness himself, the Pope. As Pope John Paul II
entered the church that morning, I tell you the people melted, swooned,
prayed, and cried. I can only conclude that there is no comparative experience

like it on this earth. The aisles of the basilica were filled with raw emotion and the very essence of the Catholic faith. People looked on at the procession in awe and chanted softly, "*IL PAPA*," as he passed down the aisle.

The aged Pontiff was dressed in all his glory and befitting the occasion. He was wearing a deep-purple cassock with gold trim and a rich, multi-colored insignia. On his head, he wore a pious white, cone-like hat, referred to in the secular world as a miter. As I stared intently at him from a distance, it was readily apparent that his age and medical conditions had taken their toll. At first glance, he looked every bit his eighty years and very unsteady. His head and shoulders leaned forward badly due to a dowager's hump—a crippling condition often associated with age. Also, his hands appeared to be trembling in periodic spasms. Rumors had long circulated that the Pope suffered from Parkinson's disease. Ironically, perhaps, he too was disabled. Many in the crowd, I'm sure, were wondering whether he was up to the anticipated tasks of the day.

As his convoy passed directly to my left, I could suddenly see his face up close. There I perceived a bold discernible strength, like the strength of many men. Instantly, I could sense and understand there was something truly exceptional about this man. There was a divine holiness about him and, at the same time, a fierce inner fortitude. There was visibly a power in his presence. He was not only the symbolic focal point of the Roman Catholic Church, standing in the shoes of the first Pope, St. Peter; but this simple, humble man from a small town in Poland was God's messenger, leading God's people and preaching God's word on earth. During his twenty-three year term up to that point, he had molded both policy and procedure, making changes throughout the world. The lives of many had improved because of him. He had changed the world with prayers and love, rather than threats and weapons. He was a leader of millions and faith was his army. As he passed by me, I was mesmerized. I could not take my eyes off him.

⌇

The intense spiritual significance of the moment somehow jolted my thoughts back to the trials and tribulations of the last six years, which had brought me here this day. There had been four major surgeries, twenty-four hospitalizations, and numerous 911 emergency calls to the ambulance squad because of violent seizures or a raging high temperature where breathing had also become an issue. In addition, there were all the doctors, nurses, battles with insurance companies, medicines, therapists, medical aides, medical appointments, a wooden stander to promote leg strength, metal walkers, and a cranial molding helmet—all to a small child barely thirty-five pounds.

By the age of four, due to recurrent ER medical treatments, she had scarred every accessible vein in her hands and feet from all the IVs necessary over that time. In the one operation alone, she had lost all the blood in her body—four pints in total. That was the worst one—the cranial vault expansion surgery—where they had to break her skull into pieces to relieve the pressure and then they re-assembled her head in order to give the brain room to grow. The plastic surgeon built a bridge from one skull plate to the other. As a parent, I'm not sure what was more painful—hearing the doctors describe the procedure beforehand or seeing the 240 stitches in her shaven little head afterward. She was, by far, the toughest person I knew. She had been through more in six years than most people could ever imagine.

∾

All that suffering, though, now seemed inconsequential as I looked forward to the altar and tried to see my wife with our special needs child, who was in the first seat of the very first pew. Through the massive crowd, I could only see the white stockings our daughter was wearing. The collective efforts of many in our group vying beforehand for optimum seating had somehow made their way through the channels and ultimately been successful. As a result, two of "my girls" were only twenty feet from the Pope as he walked onto the altar and began the opening prayer of the Millennium Jubilee Mass for the Disabled in the year A.D. 2000. It was the first time in the history of the Church that a Mass of this type had ever taken place. The Jubilee for the Disabled was part of the Church's elaborate Jubilee year festivities—a jubilee year technically occurring every twenty-five years in the Roman Catholic faith. This was, in fact, the one thousand year jubilee. This special Mass was attended by handicapped people from all over the world. Disabled adults and children had traveled with their families from around the globe to Rome for this unique day for "special needs individuals."

Our daughter had been selected by the Archdiocese of Philadelphia to be one of five lucky children to go to Italy for the seven-day pilgrimage, all centered around this special Mass. When she was three years of age, we had reluctantly placed her in a Catholic residential care facility for severely handicapped children—an enormously difficult, but necessary decision. The insensitive might refer to it as an institution, but we called it her "school." We rationalized that it was like sending your child to the best college or educational boarding program you could find, just at a much earlier age. The facility was run by a religious order of nuns dedicated to helping the sick and the less fortunate of God's children. At the facility, they had around the clock nurses and medical aides, for which our fragile daughter had a dire and constant need. In general, she attended school during the week and came home on the weekends and holidays. We needed the week to rest up. Her care was really a job for four people around the clock.

At her school, she made truly incredible progress. She received various types of daily therapy with minor, but attainable goals. Over time, they had her standing on her own and walking short distances with the aid of a metal walker apparatus. She was learning new words every day and using her very limited vision to the fullest. She had already surpassed all of the initial expectations given by the doctors. Now, here she was in Rome—an ambassador for children and adults like her all over the world.

⤜⤛

Webster's Collegiate Dictionary (Tenth Edition) - Grace:
1 a) unmerited divine assistance given man for his regeneration or sanctification,
1 b) a virtue coming from God, 1 c) a state of sanctification enjoyed through divine grace
2 d) disposition to or an act or instance of kindness, courtesy, or clemency;
3 a) a charming or attractive characteristic,
3 b) a pleasantly graceful appearance or effect;
5 a) a short prayer at a meal asking a blessing or giving thanks;
6) three sister Goddesses in Greek mythology who are the givers of charm and beauty;
8 b) the quality or state of being considerate or thoughtful.
Also...*to confer dignity or honor on; charm; favor; thanks.* (Selected text only.)

My wife and I both called her our "angel," not only because she looked like an angel to us, but also because she affected people like no child or adult we'd ever seen. We were certainly blessed that she was such a beautiful child. That was a fact. Somehow, it made all her handicaps and frailties a little easier to deal with. Many children who are severely disabled are tough for the outside world to look at. They often have such grave physical disfigurements that many folks keep a distance. While all children are beautiful in the eyes of God, the eyes of society approach things differently. Fortunately for us, our daughter made people stare in amazement at her beauty—often, I think, wondering what she would be like if she were "normal." It was kind of a cruel, bittersweet, double-edged sword. Of course, what exactly is normal when you really think about it?

There was no disputing that our little daughter had a distinct spiritual energy and special charm about her. She had a God-given charisma that captured people. She was always laughing in her soft sweet voice and providing entertainment in her own little unique way–a personality victimized by nature with ill health, but seemingly stronger as a result. People who hugged her said it made *them* feel better. Many who met her thanked us for the privilege. Some of that, of course, was people being nice; but, her interaction abilities were truly remarkable. When she learned a new word, the phrase became part of a dialogue routine. She constantly mimicked the conversation around her and, often, with poetic timing. Her word association skills were fascinating and left both a puzzled look and a chuckling smile on many a face. She memorized the words and rhythms from her favorite nursery rhymes, sung to her by so many. She also clapped her hands in sync with the music or the blurting out of timely phrases as if she understood far more than we knew. She loved prayers and songs. One time, during a Mass at her school, at the end of the priest's homily, she on her own declared, "That's nice." Things just didn't seem to be a total coincidence with her. Further, she could sense her own achievements. She knew who people were and what they did for her. Her favorite routine as a child was making the noise of bumblebees and exchanging "buzz" sounds with her many buddies for fun. She later learned to recite the alphabet, which she loved to do, taking turns with the letters with someone as it went. She got particularly excited when it came to the end with the letter "Z." The simple happiness she derived from interaction with others was astounding and uplifting. Or, maybe, there is just something very innocent and pure about a severely handicapped child who does not disobey, never complains, and cannot ever sin.

More than anything, though, people loved her and they received her unconditional love in return. I was repeatedly amazed how those who helped with her daily care (literally dozens of medical aides, therapists, doctors, nurses, pharmacy delivery men, and other care providers) often centered their entire day around her schedule, planning allotted free time to play with her, if possible. It just seemed that people became *better* people after meeting her. Many of our friends and family often came to visit her when *they* needed a break from their own stressful lives.

The Pope began the homily that fateful day as thousands sat in the balance. The message—conveyed in five different languages—was that society on a whole and through each individual should be more responsible for the disabled. It was powerful. I sat there in awe, like those around me, taking his words and invitation to heart. I pondered in silence that day in the Basilica of St. Paul's Outside the Walls in Rome, Italy. I thought about God and His place in my own life. I watched from a distance as my little angel, along with her dutiful mother, prayed within a few feet of the Pope.

Suddenly, it dawned on me that, perhaps, our daughter's life was for a reason that I might not fully understand...greater purpose, a bigger plan. With this deep reflection, the years of hardship were washed away and a renewed strength for the future was formed.

At the consecration part of the Mass a most amazing thing happened, even for this special day. When the Pope was raising the Body of Christ in the Chalice, as is custom and sacrament, at that exact moment in time, I noticed an unmistakable beam of sunlight shooting through the stained-glass windows from up above and shining directly down upon the Pope in his prayers. Gasps could be heard throughout the basilica as many others noticed the same thing all at once. For those that inquire about the existence of the Holy Spirit in our lives and the role played in the Trinity of the Catholic faith, the sunbeam took on its own identity. For others, it was simply inexplicable.

I watched as the sunbeam's life followed its own path and eventually ended, leaving the church and transcending back into the sky. The brief, unique moment passed and was gone. With that, I blinked and started reflecting on the events of the past few days in Rome leading up to this occasion. Unfortunately, our special daughter had not handled the eight-hour flight over the Atlantic Ocean as well as we had hoped. At one point, we didn't think she was going to be able to make the big Mass at all. During our third day in Rome, we had considered admitting her to the local hospital because she was becoming extremely dehydrated. She was also throwing up and, therefore, her medications, her water totals, and her feedings were off the usual schedule. The poor kid needed seventeen doses of medicine a day when she was healthy (six different medicines given via oral syringe doses throughout the day) and, if she threw up, we had to decide whether to re-dose again or not. Her sole source of food was still formula at this point in her life—given using a baby bottle—and she had a very finicky appetite on a good day, when all was going well. She couldn't eat solid foods because of her disabilities. She was orally defensive and had trouble swallowing lumpy textures. So, here she was, totally out of her usual environment and off her normal schedule...not a good combination.

Luckily for us, the two nurses traveling with our group were not only dedicated to their profession, but they thought the world of our little daughter. As the one nurse so fittingly and selflessly put it, "I can come to Rome another time. But, I want this child to enjoy the big day." *A most considerate statement*, I thought to myself at the time. Overall, several individuals in our group sacrificed their own once-in-a-lifetime working vacations to Rome, Italy, in order to help our daughter with all her needs. She was clearly their "cause," too. Together, we did everything we could to keep her strong and out of the Italian hospitals.

The glorious Mass of a lifetime ended with the Recessional hymn, sung softly by the emotional congregation. The Pope left in the same pious fashion in which he had entered. Afterwards, slowly, the thousands filtered out of the basilica. Many clearly did not want to leave. Like sports fans after a big game, the observers emptied the church with the replays stuck in our minds, not wanting the celebration to end. After months of planning and expectations, the two-hour Millennium Jubilee Mass was over all too quickly.

✁

Our group from Philadelphia now had a short afternoon break before the Papal Audience event scheduled for that evening. The audience, we were told, was an opportunity to see the Pope up closer and with entertainment provided, comparable to a Broadway show. So we all made our way in small groups back to the convent, turned bed and breakfast, where we were staying, for a brief, mid-day respite. The kids needed to be changed, fed, and cared for, and everyone welcomed some rest. It had been a long day already and for some of us, there was still a show to see.

On the walk back to the convent, my wife and I noticed a group of twenty or so nuns, dressed in their customary black habits, coming in the opposite direction on the sidewalk headed toward St. Peter's Square. As they drew closer to us, several of the nuns started pointing and talking with a heightened excitement. We were in front of the *Castel Saint Angelo* (the Castle of the Angels) on one of the bridges, which crossed over the Tiber River, when our two groups essentially reached each other. The Tiber River runs through the heart of the city of Rome and every few blocks or so, there was a bridge running over it. The nuns all surrounded our special little daughter, whom I was now pushing in her wheelchair. I quickly realized that they knew her! We soon learned that they were from the motherhouse for the very same order of nuns that ran our daughter's school. The motherhouse was located in Delaware County, Pennsylvania, just outside Philadelphia. The nuns had met our daughter when she was at the motherhouse once as a guest for dinner. The nuns greeted our daughter, showering her with hugs and kisses. We were amazed.

∽⚬⚭

In literature and religious textbooks, "grace" is often described as either the essence of grace or the existential state of grace. The essence of grace can be habitual and actual, as well as involving predestination and purification. The existential state of grace follows the path from Adam's earthly paradise, depicting grace with nature throughout history and portrays grace as it exists today within the Roman Catholic Church.

Later that day, our group from Philadelphia headed to the Papal Audience Hall, which was located to the immediate left of St. Peter's Basilica and near the Vatican's Business Center. We were some of the very fortunate to have tickets. Walking through St. Peter's Square to get there, was compelling enough in itself. At the center of the famous square, stood an Egyptian obelisk, eighty-two feet high, physically brought to Rome in A.D. 37 by Roman Emperor Caligula. Surrounding the obelisk were 284 Doric columns constructed by the sculptor Bernini during the period from 1656 to 1667. The rows of columns encircled the obelisk, each three deep and symmetrically perfect. It was an engineering marvel. It was explained to us that if you stood in the center near the obelisk, all the columns of St. Peter's Square were lined up in perfect unison, therefore, demonstrating man's harmony with life when God is at the center of our existence. As a person stood farther away from the axis, the columns became in disarray and out of focus—symbolically, the result of man without religion. On top of the columns, of course, stood the statues of all the Catholic Saints, looking down upon the masses who gathered in St. Peter's Square.

From the center of St. Peter's Square, we looked up to see the Pope's private residence, which was in the building immediately to the right, if facing the Vatican. We were told, his apartment was the only room on that entire floor of the building permitted to have a light on at night. We envisioned in our minds and reminisced from TV footage how he often greeted the people from his open window.

The Audience Hall that day was filled with six thousand people for the papal appearance and the festival. The most severely handicapped individuals were in wheelchairs up closer to the stage, with one caregiver allotted for each. This included our daughter. The rest of the crowd was seated in the back portion of the auditorium. The Pope was expected to make an entrance, starting from the back, proceed through the crowd to the front, and then watch the scheduled entertainment along with the crowd. We were informed that some of the acts would be famous Italian singers and dancers; while other parts of the show, would be performed by handicapped individuals from various countries around the world. Full of anticipation, we made our way to our assigned seats and we waited for everything to start. For the audience event, it was my turn to sit up front.

∽◌◌∽

At exactly 5:00 P.M., the Holy Father, Pope John Paul II, entered the Audience Hall. He was flanked on both sides by his papal security guards, known as the Swiss Guard. The Pope was standing on a rolling mobile platform, which had brass bars around him at shoulder height and he was being pushed deliberately and slowly by his guards. His grand entrance was accompanied by the glorious music of the Italian symphony now playing on the stage. The splendor of the procession overcame the crowd.

Slowly, the Pope proceeded from the back of the hall and down the main aisle toward the stage. The Pope's mobile platform kept moving from one side of the wide aisle to the other as he made his way. His large white chair was waiting for him, set like a throne, up close to the stage. He waved and greeted the people at the end of the rows as he went. The Pope reached out for all the extended hands and the tops of peoples' heads as he floated down the aisle. The lucky few were touched by his Holiness. Periodically, the Pope would bless the crowd as a group. He was not as young as he used to be, and it showed, but he gave the people all the energy that he had.

As the Pope came nearer to my row, I realized my unfavorable position in the middle. So, I thought I might as well try. So, I lifted our daughter out of her wheelchair and moved to get us closer to the end of the aisle. Since our row was mostly wheelchairs, I was able to make some progress.

Our little girl was certainly dressed for the occasion. She was wearing her adorable red-velvet Christmas dress with the pretty bows and white lace. She also had cute white stockings on and small, black "Mary Jane" shoes. In addition, she was a little heavier than usual. Earlier that morning, I had placed sixteen Rosary beads in a travel money belt, which we wrapped around her waist underneath her dress. My rather presumptuous and extremely optimistic plan was to distribute the rosary beads when I returned home. I figured *if* she got anywhere close to the Pope, I would consider the beads blessed and give them out to people that I knew had a handicapped child or someone sick in their family.

So, with my daughter securely in my arms and just like the throngs of the masses around me; I pushed, finagled, and positioned myself as best I could. I, too, hoped that she would somehow be touched or blessed as he passed.

Unfortunately for us, the procession was on the wrong side of the aisle and the chances were not looking good at all. The papal guards were yelling at everyone to get back. The crowd was loud and clamoring with excitement. Several people were blocking my way and things were happening fast and furious. Caught up in the moment, I kept jockeying for space. I figured we'd traveled so far and we were so close. "It" would mean so much.

I could hear behind me the other members from our Philadelphia contingent urging me to get her even closer. Actually, in truth, they were screaming at me. With that, a sense of the urgency of the moment filled my mind and soul. At that exact point in time, it struck me that I would never again in my life be in this position. This was certainly a-once-in-a-lifetime opportunity.

For some reason, at this juncture, I looked to the back of the great hall, searching for my wife and younger daughter Shannon, who were with the rest of our group in the regular seats. I caught a glimpse of my dear spouse amongst the crowd. She smiled and waved me on. She, more than anyone, deserved to be here in Rome, this day. She had been through so much. The father in a situation like ours often has his job to provide a barrier and break, but the mother of an "involved" child carries the daily burdens—both physically and emotionally. With those thoughts swarming in my mind, I stepped out a little farther. Soon, I found myself standing at the end of the aisle.

Right then, much to my surprise, the papal caravan abruptly changed course and was being steered right in my direction. This time, a different security guard was now walking toward me. He pointed at me with purpose. I prepared for another scolding or instruction to get back. Instead, to my amazement, in a deliberate tone—part broken English and part Italian—the security guard said the words I will take with me to my grave. He said firmly, "Give her to me." With that, the Pope's papal guard gently took our daughter out of my arms and walked with her out in front of the Pope's mobile platform. As he did, the entire procession came to a complete halt. Time, for me, seemed to stop. I could sense the eyes of the enormous crowd all around me, all focusing now on our daughter. Carefully, the guard handed our handicapped child up to the Pope. My heart was jumping out of my chest. Tears started rolling uncontrollably down my face. My deepest, purest dream was coming true.

That evening, Pope John Paul II managed to pick up our little angel. He paused with her in his arms and he looked her straight in the face. It appeared to me that he could tell there was something truly special about her. He connected with her…I swear it. In that instance, I felt like she epitomized what the entire day was all about and that he, more than anyone, knew it. He kissed her tenderly on the cheek and he hugged her with both his hands wrapped warmly around her neck. Then, with the help of his guards, he lifted her up again, much like a chalice gets raised during the Mass and he blessed her with the sign of the cross. After that, he delicately lowered her back down to the crowd, following her as she was returned to me. His eyes stayed fixed on her as she came back into my arms. At that moment, he blessed her again, blessing me, too, if I perceived it correctly. It was as special a moment as I could ever imagine. I had chills running down my spine. I could barely stand.

Our faithful group from Philadelphia was absolutely elated beyond words. They were jumping for joy all around me and yelling our daughter's name for all of Italy to hear. They, too, were awash with tears and shook with raw emotions. They reacted and celebrated as if she was their own child. In some ways, I've come to believe she is.

Overwhelmed, I made my way back to my designated seat and sat down, placing my arms firmly around my six-year-old daughter…hugging her. I was, perhaps, in shock. It was, I believe, pure happiness. I was full of joy and emotionally exhausted at the same time. Also, there was a sense of a mission being accomplished. It was a monumental feeling I will never forget.

After the Papal Audience was officially over that night, I continued to sit in my seat. People from around the room came over to touch our daughter, to meet her, and to embrace her. People I didn't even know. They had witnessed what I had seen. They wanted to meet the little angel with the golden hair who had stopped the procession—the little girl that the Pope had chosen from the crowd. They wanted Grace.

TOUCHED BY GRACE

"Touched by Grace" is a short story presented using a series of sixteen vignettes. The vignettes each have a specific title and are written through the viewpoint of Grace's father, who is an attorney. The brief literary sketches are based on actual events and collectively tell the story of the sixteen rosaries that Grace had on her person when she was hugged and blessed by Pope John Paul II.

One - The Ripple Effect

People generally suffer for reasons unclear to the eyes of man. God's selection process could be random, intentional, or pure fate…depending on your particular belief. But any way you look at it, the pain of life often carries with it no certain answers. However, over time, a wonderful thing can eventually result from the pain one suffers; and often that something good can heal exponentially.

"Hello there, Paula, good to see you," I said, with some emotion building in my voice as I walked from my personal office out into the main lobby. "Please, come on back," I added. As I spoke the words, I led my two o'clock guardianship matter appointment into my office. The intention was to work on the annual guardianship reports, which needed to be filed with the court. My office was cluttered and full of files, many piled high with recent mail attached on the top. I was still digging out from under—the expected result of a ten-day long vacation to Rome, Italy.

"I can hardly wait to hear about your trip," said Paula, as we walked together into my office. "Please tell me, how was Rome?"

"Our trip was absolutely incredible," I replied, with an obvious glowing pride. "Please, sit down. I actually have a video from the Papal Audience that I would like to show you. But first, let me tell you about the biggest highlight of our trip."

With that, Grace's magical encounter with the Pope was re-told in the already much traveled arrangement. Tears soon ran uncontrollably down Paula's face as she processed the story in her own particular way. She then experienced the inspirational and moving occurrence all over again by watching the incredible videotape of Grace's big moment, which had been taken by one of the people in our pilgrimage group.

"There are more tissues behind you on the credenza," I said to Paula, as I turned off the video player and sat back down in my high back lawyer chair behind my desk. "And, I have something for you when you're ready. Actually, it's a small gift for your son Kevin. By the way, how is your Kevin doing?"

"Unfortunately," she said, as she dabbed the corner of her eyes with a tissue, "not too good. He's been in and out of the hospital again." In between small sniffles that were now coming somewhat under control, Paula continued. "Last week was a real bad time. He had a nasty, fifteen-minute long seizure. But on a good note, the new medicine is helping some. Of course, it's all very frustrating. You know how it is…he is *so* involved. The folks at the state-run MR facilities do their best, but there is always something going wrong."

I nodded my head in a confirming fashion and tried to show the appropriate amount of compassion. We had entangled these heavily-laden discussions together many times before. The only comfort sometimes was to talk to someone who could relate. Paula knew that I could relate.

In time I changed the topic, "Well, my wife and I would like you and Kevin to have one of the rosaries that Grace was wearing at the Papal Audience."

A look of disbelief came over Paula's face as she fumbled for words to respond. "Oh, my goodness…. Do you mean it? The rosary beads…they've been blessed by the Pope." A short pause ensued, caused by another wave of pure, unbridled emotion, which slowed the conversation to a standstill and, seemingly, the clock on the wall, as well. Both of us now tried to regain our composure.

"Here, let me get you some more tissues; I think I might need some for myself, too," I said, as I fought to let any impulses pass before I spoke again. "Yes, I mean it. With all that you've been through in your Kevin's thirty-five years, you deserve a little positive blessing. Plus, you've been an inspiration to my wife and me. We really want you have one." I then reached to the side of my desk and pulled out one of the small gift boxes that were packed in a brand new Italian leather briefcase I possessed. In a short time, Paula had un-wrapped the tiny box and was holding the sparkling, ruby-colored beads in her hands. The long line of beads lead to a small silver cross, marked in Italian: *JUBILEE DISABLE*.

"I don't know what to say," Paula went on. "I'm speechless." We both laughed a little at that remark, because Paula was a notorious, self-proclaimed excessive talker.

"No need to say anything, Paula," I answered back. "As you've heard me say before we went on the trip, our Grace was somehow picked to go to Rome as an ambassador for *all* the handicapped in the Philadelphia area. What happened to her there is…well…it's something to be shared."

∾

Two - The Caregiver

In an emergency situation, such as we're told when on an airplane, it is standard operating procedure to grab an oxygen mask first for yourself, put it on, and then to try to help those around you.

"Your next appointment is here," spoke one of our office secretaries, Maryann, using the office intercom. "It's the elderly gentleman who wants to talk to you again about his wife going into a nursing home. He knows your Uncle Mike, the priest."

"Thank you, Maryann," I replied. "Please, would you go out to the lobby and ask him to come on back to my office." I put down the receiver and stood up, getting ready to extend a cordial greeting from behind my desk.

"Good morning, Mr. Johnson," I said, as the client walked in the office.

"Please, counselor. As I've said before, please call me Frank."

"Okay, Frank, how are you today? And how is your wife? Have you made any decisions yet?" With that, Frank sat down in one of the client chairs located in front of the desk. He looked like a man who wanted to let it all out. He was a client for wills, estate planning documents, and for elder law planning.

"Well, as you know," he said, then stopped and took a deep sigh before continuing, "I've been taking care of my Eleanor at home for several years now and the Alzheimer's is getting progressively worse. Our family doctor told me again the other day…that if I don't make the move, *I'm* likely to have another heart attack. I know what needs to be done, but she gets upset when we discuss it. She tells me I'm abandoning her. It's tearing me apart. I know I've got legal power of attorney for her and everything, but I feel so damn guilty. Before we go any further, though, how is our little Gracie doing? You know I pray for her every day when I go to morning Mass."

"Our little Grace is doing quite well, Frank, thank you," I informed him. "I have a story to tell you. In addition to that, I have a small gift for you and your wife."

"Oh, yeah, that's right. Did you go on the trip to Rome, yet? Wasn't that supposed to be this month?"

"Yes, in fact, we just got back a few days ago. Here, Frank, this is a gift for you and your wife. It's to help you deal with your difficult dilemma. It's just a set of simple rosary beads, but wait until you hear the story behind them."

"I can't accept this," he said after he heard the story. "I...."

I interrupted him. "It's no big deal, Frank, really. I was thinking of certain people when I was over in Rome and you were one of those people. They get you to pray a lot, you know, when you're staying in a convent full of nuns, down the road from the Vatican. Anyway, I figured that the rosary might give you a little boost."

∽∾∽

Three - Thank You, Doctor

I'll never forget the conversation for as long as I live. It was back in the first week of November in 1994, just a few days after our Grace was born. Her head was swollen to the size of a basketball because of all the cerebral fluid built up, all as a result of the hydrocephalus.

"Doctor, could you please explain that all to me again?" I asked and before she could even answer, I added, "The other hospital, where Grace was delivered, they want us to do surgery procedure type 'A' immediately. She is currently in their neonatal intensive care unit. As you know, I came to you for a second opinion. I've been told that you're the best pediatric neurosurgeon in the entire city. You now tell me she needs to have surgery type 'B' instead. I hear you, believe me, I do. And, I'm ready to have her transported over by ambulance immediately, but could you explain the differences one more time, please?"

"Sure," the doctor replied patiently. "If they perform surgery type 'A' on your little baby, the skull plates will collapse much too quickly when the spinal fluid is drained off so dramatically. Surgery 'A' is for older children and for adults with hydrocephalus…not for newborns. Since this is strictly a children's hospital, I can tell you from experience that surgery 'B' will allow for the plates to mold and reset better because we will drain the fluid more gradually by taking it down into the stomach. You see, an infant's skull has barely hardened at all yet, so you have to be very careful. Things have to be done slowly. Surgery 'A' will most likely deform Grace's head terribly forever and inhibit any real chance for the brain to rebound after the cerebral ventricular shunt is surgically inserted. In my opinion, it could be a catastrophe to perform surgery 'A'."

"How come the other hospital didn't say anything to us about the surgery 'B' method, doctor?" I asked. "They only discussed the one option?"

"Well, that's probably because they don't see too many of these cases with very young children. We deal with these procedures all the time, unfortunately."

Six Years Later…

"Honey, did you remember to mail a picture of Grace with the Pope along with a set of the rosary beads to Grace's neurosurgeon?" my wife asked, yelling from the kitchen into the living room, where I was sitting and watching a ballgame on TV.

"Yes, I did," I replied, as I turned my head toward her and then back to face the television. "I most certainly did."

❧

Four - The Wake

A terminal illness can be somewhat like being in the eye of a hurricane—the chartered past and the future course are both quite wicked, while any temporary calm is misleading and fleeting. But some time is nonetheless provided to prepare.

I entered the back of the receiving line that dark, rainy, January morning, thinking about what I intended to say when I eventually arrived at the family standing next to the casket. As I followed the other people in the line, I squeezed the Mass card in my fingers. I then placed the card down on top of the designated table and signed the guest registry book. I also took a eulogy card and quickly read the words of remembrance, silently to myself. After that,

I simply followed all the others, walking in a trance of sorts and doing my best to appreciate the pegboards of wonderful family pictures scattered along the way. As I approached the large bouquets of standing flower arrangements with wreaths and just after that, the family, I became nervous and almost a little nauseous. I said a quick prayer to give myself the wisdom to know what to say. The funeral was for the wife of a business client, a lovely lady. She had died after a long battle with cancer.

"I'm so sorry for your loss, Mr. Bellino," I said softly to the distraught husband when I finally reached him. "I don't know what else to say, sir." He looked exhausted.

"Thank you for your kind words, young man," the widower said back slowly, sounding weak. Then garnering a little strength, he added, "At least she isn't suffering anymore. She's finally at peace."

After that awkward somber exchange which, perhaps, is as much a part of life as life itself, I started to move slowly past the distraught husband toward his children and on the way toward the coffin. At that point, Mr. Bellino turned his head and spoke out to his four children who stood beside him, assembled by age.

"Kids…this is my business attorney, the one I told you about. This is Grace's father." As he spoke the words, I could see the eyes of their suffering faces light up a little and have a brief moment of relief, like a spot of sunshine on an otherwise dismal day. Almost all at once they inquired together, "Grace, the little girl who was hugged by the Pope?"

"Yes," I said solemnly, but assertively. I also nodded, with a growing sense of pride in the ability to make a small difference in this sometimes harsh, difficult world. As my head was automatically making its way upwards and downwards, I had a flashback to that cold December afternoon, the week right after I had returned from Rome, when I had stopped to see Mrs. Bellino at their house. That was the day I had given her one of the rosaries. It had only been a month or so since then. I remembered how she had been so fragile and thin that day with gray skin. She looked so tired and weak and had a baseball cap on her head to conceal her lack of hair. The cancer had decimated her entire body.

"You should know, counselor," spoke out the oldest son standing straight as a pillar and clearly trying to control his emotions. "Our mother requested that she be buried with those rosary beads in her hands. She has them with her right now in the casket. She was *so* proud of them." The eldest son stopped to raise a tissue to the corners of his eyes. Then he continued, "That was all she talked about whenever people came to see her in the hospital at the end. She used to say to everyone, 'Come here. Touch my rosary beads…they've been blessed by the Pope.' Sir, you have no idea how much peace they brought her. She believed that receiving those rosary beads, especially when she did, was a sign from God and prepared her for what laid ahead. Our whole family would just like to thank you from the bottom of our hearts for your thoughtfulness."

At that point, I fumbled for the right words to say and managed to reply, "I will keep you all in my prayers." That was the one line I had contemplated over and over again earlier in the receiving line.

⌘

Five - Till Death Do Us Part

When older married people think of wedding vows, two principal thoughts could come to mind. The first is that if someone actually explained the vows to young couples before the wedding, providing examples of the what-ifs of life or specific illustrations of things that can happen, a whole lot of engagements would probably meet an early demise. People just don't think that life's troubles and real problems are going to happen to them. The second, more prevailing thought though, is that without a partner to go through life, without someone to help you face the trials and tribulations that wreak their havoc, many people might not be able to travel the roads of life at all.

A black van made its way into our law office driveway and parked close to the front sidewalk. In a short time, the van's big side door slid back on its tracks and a large metal platform slowly lowered vertically to the car floor level, by use of a hydraulic lever inside the van. Once the platform was flush with the side of the van, Big Joey in his wheelchair became visible. He wheeled himself out of the van onto the platform and then gave his wife, Janet, the thumbs up signal, in order for the platform to be lowered down to street level. The noise of the hydraulic lift pierced through the mild winter afternoon air, drawing the attention of anyone entering any of the nearby businesses. After a few more seconds that for some reason seemed much longer, the platform landed down on the asphalt driveway with a thud. Big Joey then un-strapped his wheelchair from the lift safety binders and rolled himself onto the driveway. There, he waited for his wife to return the lift and close the sliding door.

After that was all done, they started together toward the front door of the law office for their four o'clock appointment with her pushing his wheelchair. They had called me a week back about an estate for someone who had died on Joey's side of the family. Big Joey was apparently the named executor in the Will. His wife, Janet, pushed him up the handicapped ramp and into the office.

Big Joey was forty-eight years old and suffered from MS. He had thinning blonde hair, a ruddy complexion, and was severely underweight due to all the complications associated with his medical condition. For him, every meal came through a feeding tube—a precarious and difficult plight, according to his wife. All he did every day now, according to Janet, was watch TV and take medicine. His story was both sad and surreal. He had been first diagnosed with MS in his late twenties, which was, of course, a terrible shock to everyone. There had been no prior signs or warnings at all. He had always been a healthy guy. He had played sports and enjoyed the outdoors. After graduating high school, he served his country in the Army for two years and even received a medal for bravery. The Army had helped him attain a college education by going to night school, while he worked during the day. His chosen occupation became accounting. Right when he became sick the first time, he had just started moving up in the company. He used to play softball on Friday nights with the guys in the neighborhood and loved working around the house on weekends. These days, his wife and three children had to do everything for him.

Joey's wife, Janet, had first met our Grace when she was just an infant. It was about a month after Grace had the initial cerebral shunt surgery and had been released from the hospital. Grace's doctors all recommended a nurse's aide to help my wife at home with all the care involved. That's where Janet came in. She worked, at the time, for the local hospital out-source home care staff. She became the designated aide assigned to Grace and our family. The assignment was something, Janet often said, that changed her life.

"I told Joey that something special would happen to Grace in Rome," Janet exclaimed, after being told about the events of the special trip. "Didn't I, Joe?" She looked over at her husband for confirmation and then continued, "I knew that somehow, some way, Grace, of all the kids, of all the people there, somehow she would get close to the Pope. I can't believe it happened, but I'm not surprised one bit. There is just something very special about Grace." Janet had always been one to wear her emotions on her sleeve and to speak her mind. This occasion was certainly no different.

"I know," I said back. "We feel the same way. It was incredible. Now here, Janet, please take this rosary. It's for you."

With that, Janet took hold of the rosary beads handed to her like someone grabs onto a rope if they are near a dangerous cliff. Her eyes welled up and tears started running uncontrollably down her face.

"Janet, let me add, that you, as much as anyone, deserves to share in Grace's big moment. If it wasn't for your help during those early years, I don't know where we'd be now. Grace probably would never have made it through and my wife and I would, most likely, would be running around with straight-jackets in padded rooms. We owe you a lot and we consider you a part of our family."

∽∽

Six - Against the Odds

The flight to Italy reminded me a lot of Grace's life on the whole—it was extremely involved and difficult. We had eight long, uncomfortable hours on the plane, hardly any room to move around, and we couldn't sleep. To make matters worse, our Grace wasn't feeling well. She kept throwing up anything we gave her to drink or eat. She started to look peaked and was acting lethargic, which was always a dangerous sign with her. The nurses on the trip were already concerned that she might be getting dehydrated. That's the last thing I ever thought of—God forbid, Grace had to be hospitalized in Rome. What a mess that would probably be. The biggest concern was if she spiked a fever as that could cause a seizure, and when Grace had seizures, she sometimes stopped breathing. That was why we always carried a portable oxygen tank with us everywhere we went. It all reminded me of what I often said to others about having a handicapped child in general—it's difficult and it doesn't get any easier just because you want it to.

My wife was seated to my left on the plane, near the window, with Grace in between us. I could see that my wife was already exhausted. She had just changed Grace's diaper, which is a difficult project on a changing table back at our home because of all the involved complexities. But, to change our six-year-old Grace in an airplane seat—given her size, her energy, and the vesicostomy surgical incision located below her belly button, which emptied urine constantly so to avoid urinary tract infections—was almost impossible. I noticed my wife now had her eyes closed and was holding the audience tickets firmly in her hands. I could tell she was praying, and I knew exactly what she was thinking about, too…sort of like when I arrive home after work and the pile of chores I had promised to do, were looming in the unspoken air.

I whispered to her, "Honey, please remember what my uncle, the priest, said to me on the phone the other day." I went on, "Please don't get your hopes up too much. Going to the jubilee event is special enough." My wife opened her eyes and turned toward me.

"What did Father Mike say to you again, exactly?" my wife inquired, for at least the third time in two days. She often had a distinct habit of asking me the same question several times in a short span of time. I never knew whether she had a bad memory or did it on purpose to drive home a point.

"Father Mike reminded me, dear, he reminded *us*…that the odds of our Grace getting anywhere near the Holy Father are almost impossible. My uncle's been a priest for over fifty years, been to Rome seven times, and he's never even met the Pope. In fact, he's never been in the same room as the Pope. It's not a matter of being a negative or positive thinker; it's about being practical. My uncle was just trying to be helpful. So, please, sweetheart, try to be realistic."

"All I know," she said back with rising conviction, "is that the maternity doctors said that Grace wouldn't make it through the delivery. They were wrong! Then, the delivery doctors said that she probably wouldn't live a year. They were wrong again. The one, big-shot neurologist at the first hospital, in fact, told us that she would only develop to the level of a two month-old baby mentally, and as you know, her vocabulary now has over 100 words in it. And, the first group of physical therapists we had said she would never walk and now she does. The eye doctors told us she was completely blind and now we know that she can at least see some sunlight and shapes. So, forgive me, but I just don't listen to what people say in the negative anymore about our Grace."

"Okay, okay, Honey, fine, enough; then let's hope for the best. And will you remind me, please, Father Mike asked me to buy him a set of rosary beads in the Vatican gift shop."

⟜∞⟊

Seven - Sweet as Sugar

Someone once said to me that when Grace hugs you, she makes *you* feel better. Indeed, that was a very true statement. Grace hugs people with such genuine and uncompromised affection. She seeks absolutely nothing in return and has no motive other than pure unconditional love. We can all learn from her.

One blustery winter afternoon, a month or so after our big trip to Rome, I was entering a local restaurant to meet clients. I scurried in the door to be saved from the wind, before I blew away. My clients wanted to discuss a legal matter with me over lunch. It was some kind of a boundary-line dispute with a neighbor, which apparently began when they had their property surveyed for the purpose of putting up a fence. The restaurant we had agreed upon was the vegetarian place near my office, which we all loved.

My clients, Ben and Sara, were already seated and waiting for me when I arrived. They were busy perusing the menus. They were very particular eaters; they had to be because they were diabetic. They both suffered from severe diabetes, stemming from their youth. It struck me, as I got to know them better over the years, that diabetes is not only a serious disease, but it is also extremely prevalent in our society. In fact, it is my humble opinion that diabetes is going to be a bigger and bigger problem for future generations. The simple reasons being our terrible eating habits, the large amount of food we eat these days, and all the preservatives added into our food. The trip to Italy taught me something on those issues, as well. The people in Europe eat much less than we do, and they eat only the freshest produce, breads, and dairy products—not the preserved, genetically-altered crap we stuff ourselves with. For example, just order a hoagie in Europe and you'll see what I mean. You'll think they are trying to rip you off. They give you one single slice of meat, a tiny sliver of cheese and forget the mayonnaise. But, the bread is so darn fresh, it knocks your socks off.

"Hello, *consigliore*. How was the trip to *Italiano?*" said Sara, in her usual peppy excitable manner." Her bilingual efforts were more for fun than to be taken seriously.

"Wonderful, thank you, Sara," I said back and then sat down to join them. "But, you already know the real highlights of our trip. You guys were one of the first people I called when we got back and were settled. I take it that you received the gifts I mailed."

"Yes, we did," said Sara. She was the talker of the two. Ben was the quiet professor type. He sat back and enjoyed the scenery. "First of all, we are touched beyond words." She went on, "Secondly, why didn't you just wait to give it to us? You didn't have to mail them."

"I knew Ben was going away to Canada on a business trip and I didn't want to wait. If you lived around the corner from the office, I would have dropped them off. But since you live all the way down in Delaware County, I gave the government a job to do."

"Well, Ben just loves the book marker depicting Michelangelo's Sistine Chapel and I don't know where to begin about the rosary beads blessed by the Holy Father. You know how religious I am."

"Yes, I do. That's *one* of the reasons I gave it to you. But, before we dig into the subjects of the day and review my extensive photographs from the trip, what do you guys want to eat? Let's be ready to order."

"I know what I'm going to get," spoke Ben in a soft astute tone. "Last time I had that Portobello mushroom sandwich on the Panini bread. That was out of this world. I'm getting that again."

"And it's healthy for you, too," I quipped back, sort of half-kidding. We had a running joke about the restaurant's delicious food. The rational being that anything served in a vegetarian restaurant had to be good for you, no matter how many calories and how sinful it tasted."

"Ben, we just need to inject the insulin dosages before we dine," said Sara as she looked affectionately over at her husband. With that, the two of them administered their own medication to themselves right at the table, pricking their fingers to take a reading and then using the modern insulin ports implanted in their sides. Before, I would cringe when they administered the medicine in a restaurant, but now I watched, took note, and learned.

∽∾

Eight - Never Gone

I had initially come up with the idea of buying the rosaries in Rome as a gift for certain people, when I was handling the real estate matter for Betty. She had just lost her husband of forty years and was selling the family house they'd lived in together since they were newlyweds. It was a pretty emotional time for Betty and she was trying to sell the house all by herself, without any realtors. It was while hearing Betty's stories about her handicapped, only daughter Katie—who had died many years back at the age of twelve—that I became inspired. Betty expressed such love and fond memories despite the tremendous ordeals the family had gone through because of their daughter's severe disabilities. Betty had devoted herself to her daughter who had been sick every single day of her life. Seeing the old pictures Betty brought in one day to my office almost made me cry. Some people deserve much better than the plight they get in life. Others, don't appreciate what they have until it's too late. People like Betty, though, they take whatever life offers and they make the best out of it, and they don't complain one bit. As Betty put it after the real estate settlement for her house was finally over, and I was walking her to her car outside my office, "My Katie will always be with me. She's up in heaven right now looking out for me." As Betty spoke, she pointed upward. We both looked up toward the sky and smiled.

"Diane," I said to my paralegal, on my first day back after the trip to Rome, "Would you please call Betty McClain and ask her to come in one day next week? Please explain to her that I want to tell her about our trip to Rome and about the Jubilee Mass for the Disabled. And, tell Betty if you would, that I have a little gift for her."

∽∾∽

Nine - It Is Truly a Very Small World

I have to admit being a bit surprised when I opened the letter from my old high school buddy and read the sincere, touching comments contained therein. Ever since our prankster-filled days, playing baseball together in the Philadelphia Catholic League, I had considered him one of the funniest people I'd ever met. We were battery mates back then. He was the crafty left-handed pitcher and I was the slow-footed, supposedly power-hitting catcher, although in truth I hit more long foul balls than anything else. Anyway, when we were teenagers, I never really saw his serious side, but hey, life has a way of changing people, or at least, letting us all grow up.

The letter was a thank-you note for my giving his father one of the rosaries. His father had been in the hospital due to a stroke, acute kidney failure and, according to his family, near the end. So, I visited. To me, it was simple. His father deserved a nice gesture in return for what he had done a few years prior for our daughter Grace. The story about it was always told best by my pal Donny himself when we were drinking beers together and reminiscing about the "good old days." I remember one time we had played golf together in our annual high school golf outing and the topic came up while we were standing at the bar afterward, talking with our friends.

"So go ahead, Donny, tell us the donation story," inquired our mutual friend, Billy, who had never heard it before. He had overheard Donny and I make reference to the story several times throughout the day while golfing.

"Okay, I will," Donny said. I stood and waited for him to begin. I always thought he was a great storyteller.

"Years back, my father calls downtown to the main office for the Archdiocese," Donny started out, "and my dad asks about the different organizations within Catholic Social Services that helped the handicapped in the Philadelphia area. He was feeling charitable, but he had nothing particular in mind. He just wanted the money to go to those who needed it the most."

"What did downtown say?" I asked on cue. I knew the answer, but felt compelled to help advance the story along.

"The Archdiocese recommended a donation to St. Michael's Home for medically fragile and severely handicapped children. So, on a Monday, my dad sends out a sizable check in the mail. It was no small chunk of change, I can tell you that." Donny definitely had a way with words.

"Then what happened," asked Bobby, Billy's twin brother, and another one of the regular golfers in our foursome for the annual high school alumni golf outing. We all graduated in the same year and had about the same basic ability on the golf course—we stunk. To make matters worse, though, Billy and Bobby liked to make a lot of bets with our fellow alumni who were actually very good at golf. So, our foursome usually lost a significant amount of money on bets each year.

Donny continued, "A few weeks later after making the donation, my dad gets the St. Michael's latest newsletter in the mail. On the front cover was the bold heading: 'Welcome Grace – Our Newest Resident!' My father knew who it was right away and he started to get emotional."

"Why was he emotional?" asked still another friend named Barry, who had just walked up to the bar and didn't quite understand the poignancy of the moment. Donny then looked around at all of us. With his eyes and mannerisms, he pulled us toward him to hear the answer.

"My dad got emotional," Donny said softly, "because he knew Grace was the daughter of one of my good friends. My father felt like his charitable contribution had directly helped someone he knew. He truly believed he was making a difference in the world."

We all stood there in reflection, but Donny wasn't quite finished.

"And then," Donny added, changing voice inflections and sounding like a priest fresh off the boat from Ireland delivering a powerful Sunday homily, "when my father received the rosary beads blessed by Pope John Paul II in the hospital, close to the end, my father cried."

After that, we all turned toward the bar and ordered another round of cold beers. We toasted together…in memory of Donny's dad.

Ten - Medicine for the Mind and Soul

"I thank you very much, counselor, but you realize, don't you, that my wife isn't even Catholic?" The words came out of my accountant's mouth as deliberately and calmly as everything else he did. He displayed very little emotion and was cool as a cucumber.

"Yes, I realize that," I replied. "You told me that little detail before. I just thought she might appreciate it anyway. As someone famous once said, 'It's the thought that counts.'" After making the statement, which was intended to lighten the moment, I looked my accountant straight in the eye to convey what sometimes words cannot, at least not between men for some strange reason. I knew he was worried about the possibility of losing his dear partner in life and all other things get dwarfed when a real problem besets itself.

"Oh, she'll appreciate it," he said. "And, I *very much* appreciate it. With everything that's going on—the chemo, the radiation, all the breast cancer related nightmares—we'll take any type of positive energy we can get. And this… this is definitely positive energy."

"Enough said, then, my number-crunching friend. I hope it helps. And, we'll continue to keep your wife in our prayers."

∽∾

Eleven - The Breadth of an Angel

My wife's crazy Aunt Gertrude deserves a break in life. Maybe her turn is coming, I don't know. But, I hope so. In the meantime, I worry about her and I will continue to pray for two things in her regard. The first item I pray for is her health. Ever since that bad fall, on a snow-covered, unsalted parking lot in the winter of 1994—the year that will live in infamy in my family—her health just has never been the same. Chronic back pain, hip pain, and bad knees together can be brutal and debilitating. Not too much I can do about all that anymore. The lawsuit is settled, monies received, but the residual symptoms still remain. She does contend, however, that ever since she received the rosary beads from Rome, the pain is not quite as bad. The other thought, though, that repeatedly comes to my mind with regards to my wife's Aunt Gertrude, is all the angel mementoes that she buys for our daughter Grace. I know Aunt

Gertrude is thoughtful and she loves her special great-niece as much as she possibly could, but we're running out of room in our house. We have the angel gifts everywhere. I pray that either she stops buying the angel books, angel statues, angel stickers, angel puzzles, poems about angels in frames for hanging on the wall, pillows with angel faces on them, matching angel bookends for the bookshelf, picture frames with angels in the margins, angel Christmas ornaments, paintings of angels, quilts with angels stitched on them, stuffed angel dolls, embroideries containing all the angels of distinction, angel candle holders, etc....or, that somehow I can convince my wife that we can store the stuff downstairs in the basement.

Well, that's what I pray for regarding my wife's Aunt Gertrude and we wanted her to have a rosary.

∽∾

Twelve – "Twelve"

In the Bible, there are, of course, many significant references to the number twelve which note distinction. To start with, there were twelve apostles who followed Christ and then spread the Gospel after his death. In addition, the days before Christmas count out twelve for some particular reason I never quite understood. The list goes on and on.

My wife and I decided that the twelfth rosary was a special one and had to go to her mother for all that she did for us. When Grace comes home on weekends and for holidays from St. Michaels, my mother-in-law is the one who helps us with administering the seventeen medicine doses a day, the diaper changes every two hours, the enemas, the water monitoring necessary because of Grace's bad kidneys, and the rather complicated pureed feeding efforts. In addition, when our Grace is hospitalized for whatever reason, whether it be kidney troubles, a seizure, an ear infection, another urinary tract infection, a bowel obstruction, pneumonia, a problem with the shunt, dehydration, a flu, or a bad virus, it is my dear mother-in-law who stands up to the plate and helps us out. She comes over and lives at our house for as long as needed. She watches our younger daughter Shannon while we basically live downtown at the children's hospital in shifts. So, the decision was simple for rosary number twelve. We gave that important rosary to my wonderful, always helpful, incomparable mother-in-law...but with one small condition. She had to promise to give it back to us if we ever needed it.

Thirteen - A Good Friend

A person is lucky in life to have a few truly good friends. That is a well-known premise.

I have a good friend who was born with Cystic Fibrosis. For years, no one even knew he had the disease and then, when they found out, they couldn't explain why. After a lot of tests, his life expectancy, according to all the experts, was projected to be age thirty-six. He is now in his late forties. Every day past his thirty-sixth birthday he considers a gift. He's the kind of friend that would come over right away if you called him for help. He's the kind of friend who would do anything for you if you asked. He's the kind of friend who wouldn't even ask why you wanted help. Many years ago, I gave this gentleman one of the rosaries from our Rome trip. I just hope it's helping.

∞

Fourteen - Life Can Be Hard

A client of mine, while in her early twenties, had been in a bad car accident. Her car was broadsided by a truck. She was devastated at the time with the injuries, the terrible pain, and the way the injuries limited her abilities to do her everyday activities. She still had problems even long after the medical tests and treatments were finished. The simplest of efforts were difficult for her and for a long while, she could not go to work. The lawsuit recovery eventually helped out financially, but not with the pain. In time, though, with a lot of physical therapy, she resumed her lifestyle, got married, and started a family.

Then, her only son got sick with Leukemia at the age of eight. She and her husband were devastated. None of the treatments worked and they tried them all. They traveled everywhere to different hospitals and various cities for second opinions. Their entire life became about battling the illness and they fought the battle together bravely until the boy's final breath. One item they had along the way was a rosary from our trip to Rome. I hope it gave her some comfort, some hope, some source of strength, because sometimes life can be hard.

Fifteen - A Business Association Friend

A friend of mine, a co-member of one of the many business associations that I belong to, is a deeply religious person; she goes to Mass every day and is truly a sweet lady. So, I gave her one of the rosary beads we brought back from Rome.

∽∾∽

Sixteen - The Wall

There is an old adage to throw a bunch of stuff against the wall and see what sticks. People often use a wall for a display or a shrine. A wall separates two different rooms. A wall can separate two people. A person can build up a wall within themselves. A wall can block progress. A wall can surround. A wall connects the floor to the ceiling. A wall can attack. A wall is a good defense. A wall of water can come at you. A wall can be taking things to an extreme. You can drive someone up a wall. A wall can be an interior layer. A wall protects and oversees.

We decided to keep the last rosary for Grace. It was hers. It is now hanging on a small picture hook over her bed in her bedroom at our house. It is on the wall that overlooks her bed as she sleeps when she is home.

THE LOVEBUG

She simply likes to hug people. It's an inherent, genetic quality many might say, perhaps hard for some people to understand; and probably came along with her unique individual spirituality. Since she was only twelve years old at the time, there were still a lot of unanswered questions. Certain things, however, were known. For example, she was a severely handicapped child, both physically and mentally, and she was considered legally blind. Born with a primary condition called hydrocephalus, which as it turned out was only the beginning of the full diagnosis. She had fifteen different doctors and she had been hospitalized forty-four times in her lifetime, thus far. But, despite all her medical problems, we considered her an angel from God…just an angel with a very complicated medical methodology. We, her parents, believed that all the fascinating circumstances, ironic connections, and thought-provoking occurrences were not mere coincidences. Maybe it was our faith that led us in that direction or maybe, wishful thinking. Either way, it became the fabric of our lives.

Her name was Grace and she had been born on All Saints' Day. Add to those simple circumstances the notion that she had, by all accounts, never intentionally sinned, never done anything on purpose to ever hurt anyone in her life, and the prospect became quite an interesting combination of fate and providence for those with strong religious convictions. Then, add to the building equation the next interesting component—when you looked in a book about angels, she looked *exactly* like the angel Grace depicted in the books. She had blond curly hair, light blue eyes, porcelain white skin, and red rosy cheeks.

"Daddy, how much longer until we get to the Retreat House?" asked Grace's younger sister Shannon, speaking from the back of the Volvo station wagon with Grace seated next to her. Grace kept herself busy, as usual, randomly repeating words from nursery rhymes and manipulating a long red ribbon in her hands. Grace loved to play with strings, shoe laces, and ribbons, especially while listening to music. Although it was still rather early—8:45 on a Sunday morning to be exact—the CD playing in our car was my favorite musical group—U2—and their album entitled *All That You Can't Leave Behind*. My all-time favorite song is on that CD.

Their dutiful mother was sitting in the front passenger seat and answered on my behalf, "About five more minutes, Shannon. Now, please, just be patient." Loving mom also turned around and checked the backseat to make sure all was in order with both her girls.

Shannon looked down at the Nintendo portable game on her lap and started to pay more attention to the developing heightened action, but at the same time, she asked, "Why are we going to this 'retreat thing' anyway?" She wasn't being disrespectful really, merely questioning, as kids her age often do. After all, she was only eleven.

Again Mom led the response. "The title of the retreat is called 'Women of Grace' and your father wanted us all to go. Your father read about it in *The Catholic Standard and Times* newspaper. He thought we all should go together." As mom spoke, she looked over at me driving. She didn't look entirely convinced herself.

There were no seats available in the chapel when we arrived at the Conference Center where the final retreat Mass was about to take place. Luckily, one of the thoughtful assistants noticed us standing in the outer hallway and helped us by placing four extra chairs in the front row on the right side of the church when looking at the altar. The assistant guided us to the seats and even held one of Grace's hands as we walked. Grace, although blind, did walk with supervision. She moved with a distinct awkward fashion, but could walk on her own if someone held one of her hands to show her the way. Shortly after being seated, the Mass began.

Going to Mass together as a family had become one of the our favorite family things to do together, ever since the magical, once-in-a-lifetime moment we shared in Rome, Italy, when we attended the Jubilee Millennium Mass for the Disabled in the year 2000. That day, along with 13,000 others, we had been inspired monumentally by the surprise arrival and participation in the Mass of the ailing, but resilient Pope John Paul II. Things went emotionally exponential after that at the Papal Audience following the Mass, when the Pope picked our little Grace out of a crowd of thousands, hugged her, kissed her, and blessed her.

The Mass at the Retreat House, meanwhile, was designed to be the final component of the weekend-long retreat for a group of about two hundred woman in attendance. The focus of the retreat was a Catholic woman's role in today's society and based on the teachings of Pope John Paul II. Our family knew no one there. I had called only on a whim at the last minute after reading the article about it in the Philadelphia area Catholic newspaper. I was, in fact, the only man present, except for the priest saying the Mass. I wanted my wife and daughters to attend at least part of the retreat, if possible. I had inquired and received permission for us to attend the Mass.

Together we sat through the Mass. When it came time for Communion, my wife started the usual procedure for Grace to receive the sacrament. She held Grace's hand and carried a Dixie cup of water as they walked together in line, up toward the priest along with everyone else. I followed behind in the procession and moved around at the very last second to help Grace accept the host. It was always a team effort. I whispered to the priest to give Grace a tiny sliver of the body of Christ to be put in the Dixie cup for Grace to drink. As the priest did so, Mom meanwhile sang a nursery rhyme to relax and distract Grace while also coaxing her to drink the contents of the Dixie cup. That was the only way our little Grace could receive Communion due to her disabilities, otherwise she would gag on the dry host. Grace was what they called "orally defensive" and, thus, had trouble swallowing regular foods. All her meals, in fact, had to be pureed and served with fluids. We then received Communion ourselves and we all eventually returned to our seats at the far end of the first row.

As we sat there quietly having received Communion, we watched and waited for the rest of the congregation to do the same. Many in attendance walked right in front of us as the normal communion procession continued. The procession of everyone returning to their seats then suddenly stopped, due to congestion somewhere in the line. At that point, an elderly woman with white hair and a light beige dress stood in the line in front of our seats. The woman waited there for a few seconds, standing directly in front of where our Grace was seated. For some unknown reason, Grace stood up at that exact particular moment and took a few awkward steps toward the woman. Grace then spread her arms open wide and grabbed the woman to give her a big hug. Grace gave the woman a gigantic, unsolicited, prolonged hug, which lasted for at least fifteen seconds. Grace tightened her grasp and would not let go. The woman was, of course, surprised at first, but soon enough smiled politely with a warm receiving manner and eventually just hugged Grace back. The woman even bent down at one point and gave Grace a sweet kiss on the cheek. My wife and I, meanwhile, had jumped up immediately to quickly corral little Grace back to her seat, with an air at first to apologize for the intrusion, but we could sense no offense had been taken by the woman. So, we simply smiled and eventually we garnered Grace to sit back down and the procession line continued. The elderly woman in the beige dress kept walking and headed on her way to her seat, located somewhere in the back of the chapel.

A few moments later, I felt someone behind me tapping me on my shoulder. I turned to look and found a middle-aged lady with black hair holding a set of rosary beads in her hands. She looked quite religious and very pious.

"Excuse me, sir," the woman behind me said in a quiet whisper. "But does your daughter know the elderly woman who just went by, the woman she hugged?"

I turned my head and whispered back, "No, not at all. In fact, our daughter is mentally handicapped and blind. We never know why she does certain things. She just loves to hug people." There was a slight gasp of sorts and then a silence as the woman behind me seemed to gather her thoughts in reflection in order to speak again. She soon did.

The woman leaned forward and continued, "The amazing thing, sir, is that particular lady really needed a hug. I've been attending these group retreat sessions with her all weekend and she's really quite depressed about her life. She's got a lot going on, as some really tragic things have happened to her recently."

I reflected and shook off a wave of raw emotion at the powerful spiritual implications which quickly came flooding into my mind. I then conveyed a few quick details about the transcending qualities of our unique, special needs daughter, including all the interconnections she had with the word "grace" itself and, of course, I quickly told the condensed version of the story of Grace's magical encounter with her famous friend who once lived in Rome. I expressed the conclusion that maybe Grace was passing the hug from the Pope forward. I also quoted what one family friend had once said to me about Grace: "When Grace hugs you…you feel better."

The woman seated behind me started to get emotional and replied, "Oh, wait until I tell the lady that she was hugged by an angel from God. You have no idea what that will mean to her."

Questions for the reader:

1. What does the title of the story mean?

2. On how many levels is Grace a lovebug?

The Best Gift I Could Think Of

It was Christmas Eve. I lay in my bed thinking about the exciting morning soon to come…only a few, but extremely long hours away. I tried my best to drift off to sleep, which my mother had sweetly requested when she tucked me in earlier, but I couldn't help but wonder about possible gifts under the tree and the pure magic of Christmas morning. I knew exactly what I wanted from Santa, too. I snuggled under my big fluffy Disney World comforter with such pleasant thoughts dancing in my mind while I gazed out the frosted, blurry windows of my bedroom. I noticed the shining reflections coming from our outside Christmas lights, all the time listening to the Christmas music my parents had playing downstairs in the family room. My father had made a roaring fire that evening with intense crackling flames. He'd tried, once again, to cook chestnuts in the open fire; one more year without much success, though. I loved the smell and the warmth of a fire in the wintertime. I also loved all kinds of music, especially Christmas songs. I could listen to music all day every day. We had all stood around the fireplace together and sung Christmas carols until it was my bedtime. My Gamma served all the adults homemade eggnog, while my Great Aunt Gertrude sang *White Christmas* all by herself—off-key at the top of her lungs.

"Birds, bunny rabbits, bees.… Old McDonald had a farm, E I E I O.…"

I could hear my sissy in her bedroom across the hallway. She was getting ready for bed. Her bedtime is after mine, even though she is younger than me. That doesn't bother me, though. I could hear her putting away her Christmas dress in the big closet that connects our two rooms…the dress she'd worn for Christmas Eve Mass. Our dresses had matched, as usual. They were both red and green velvet with dainty white lace collars. Our family always went to Mass on Christmas Eve, for some reason, which was fine with me because it made Christmas morning that much longer and more fun. We didn't have to rush anywhere and we could stay in our pajamas. I loved going to church too, especially on holidays.

"Birds, bunny rabbits, bees…. Twinkle, twinkle little star, how I wonder what you are…."

✌

The gift I was thinking of the most, though, was the one I wanted to give to my mother for Christmas. This year I really wanted to show her how much I loved her. My mother and I are very close and we do a lot of fun stuff together. We go shopping for clothing. We buy shoes…lots of shoes. We go for walks in the neighborhood and in flower gardens. We swim in the summertime. She absolutely loves dressing my sissy and me in all kinds of pretty outfits. On Sundays, we have family picnics together. We play wiffleball a lot with my dad and if it's raining out, we all go to the movies. I love going to the movies—all the loud noises, music, and bright lights. The movies we go to usually are the happy ones with tiny cartoon characters running around and someone eventually saving the day. At the movies, my mother always sits next to me so we can whisper and have fun together. She always makes sure I have a string in my hands to play with and plenty of water to drink. My mother really loves giving me water.

My mother is extremely important to me. I love my dad, too, of course—he's a real character; but my mom, well she's the one who always takes care of me, especially when I'm sick. She takes me to the doctors when I need to go, which unfortunately is quite a lot. She goes to school to talk with my teachers. She attends all my school functions and chaperones on my class trips. Not all the moms go, you know. Now that I'm a little older, I realize things better. After all, I'm fourteen now.

My dad calls me his little angel, which I admit I really like. He say's I'm an angel because my name is Grace, and because I was born on All Saints' Day. I think that is actually a pretty cool coincidence. Also, he tells people all the time that when you go to a book of angels and look up the "official" Angel

Grace, she looks exactly like me. My dad goes on to tell people that I have curly blond hair, white porcelain skin, rosy red cheeks, and big blue eyes. I don't know about all that stuff so much, but I like when he calls me his angel. Then, after I met Pope John Paul II in Rome, Italy, on our big trip for the special Millennium Jubilee Mass for the Disabled…well, my dad just couldn't stop telling people about me after that. That's a dad, I guess….

My mother is very pretty. She has long blond hair, a lot longer than mine. She has a beautiful smile and I guess I have her eyes because they are the same color. People say I also have her slender fingers and a low sweet voice like my mom. I have my father's nose, though, I think, and my Gamma's prominent, very lady-like chin. My mom's very patient, too. Those are just some of the reasons I hope she gets lots of good presents this year. She keeps a special photo album in the kitchen cupboard over the microwave, just with pictures of me, such as my first day of school each year, my official school send-home pictures, and pictures of me in my Halloween costumes each fall. Plus, she keeps every single school craft project I ever made.

"Birds, bees, bunny rabbits…. London Bridge is falling down, falling down, falling down…."

❧

I really want my mom to know how much I love her this particular Christmas. Unfortunately, it's hard for me to verbalize how I feel and I'm not a good writer at all. Certainly, I'm not as good a writer as my sissy. Also, I don't do well speaking in front of people. I'm not shy exactly, but people just don't always understand me. My words come out different than my thoughts, sometimes all jumbled up. I hug my mom a lot and I tell her I love her whenever I can, but I don't think it's enough. I want to explain things better. I want her to know *how much* she means to me.

"Birds, bees, bunny rabbits…. Three Blind Mice, Three Blind Mice…."

❧

Which reminds me, somewhere along the way, I heard a person say that blind people can sometimes have increased abilities with their other senses, such as the ability to hear, smell, or touch. Maybe that is true with me. I hope so anyway, especially since I'm considered "legally" blind by the doctors. I can see "some" but not very much. They also say I'm severely mentally and physically handicapped, which sounds pretty bad I guess, but I'm happy. I can walk some. Granted, I don't walk too well. I'm a little awkward and unstable, and I do fall sometimes, but that's what my helmet is for. Also, I usually need to wear my hard-plastic leg mafos during the day for support. But, all things considered, I get around pretty well. I truly love to walk, too. I know I still wear diapers, but I'm working on it. I get seventeen doses of medicine each day, for different kinds of stuff like seizures. I need to take all the medicine by syringes. I truly dislike taking all the medicine, but what can you do? I've adjusted. Also, my food needs to be pureed because I can't swallow lumpy textures. That's a lot of work for my mom. The worst part, though, I think anyway, has to be all the hospitalizations I've had. My dad says I've been hospitalized forty-eight times in my lifetime so far. I'm not complaining mind you, but it must be hard on my parents and my sissy. I know that many a holiday season has been spent with me in the hospital with serious problems. I know that much for sure. I've had urinary infections, kidney failures, bowel obstructions, ear infections, pneumonia, and my shunt sometimes gets clogs—'the whole nine yards' as my dad likes to say. And I've had four big surgeries too, some of which were pretty brutal. To be honest, I don't even like thinking about the one procedure I had—the "cranial vault expansion surgery"—that's where they broke my skull into pieces in order to relieve the pressure on my brain and my spinal column. Then, the team of doctors built some kind of bridge in my head and put my skull back together again. The surgery saved my life they said, but it certainly hurt a lot. My father says I was like Humpty-Dumpty, only much, much prettier. He counted the stitches in my head after that surgery. He said there were two hundred and forty stitches.

"Birds, bees, bunny rabbits.... Rudolph the Red Nose Reindeer...."

∾∾

The thing is...my mother never leaves my side when I'm sick, except for maybe a few minutes to get sissy ready for school. She even sleeps in my room if I'm home from school or in the hospital when I have a fever because she's afraid I'll have a seizure. So, after I got done listing in my mind all the things I wanted Santa to bring me this year for Christmas (more music tapes, more ribbons and strings for me to wrap around my fingers because I like the sensation, more stuffed animals for my bedroom, more books of nursery rhymes for people to read to me, and more matching dresses for my sissy and I to wear on special occasions), I tried to concentrate on what I could give my mother. As

I was thinking about it, my hands bumped into one of the special safety rails attached to my Vail bed and it reminded me that my mother was probably somewhere downstairs carrying the baby monitor she still uses for me and listening intently. The monitor is pretty neat, it has a little camera, too. I'd think she was being overly dramatic if it weren't for the one time I had a sudden seizure up here in bed, causing me to stop breathing. She saved my life when she rushed upstairs with the Diastat, the portable oxygen tank, and gave me CPR. She's always worrying about me. But back to Christmas gifts…of course, I made her a few things in school with help from my teacher, but my mother deserves even more than that. So, as I'm lying here now, waiting for Santa and Rudolph to land on the roof at any minute, it suddenly occurs to me that maybe the best gift I can give my mother for Christmas this year is for me simply to be healthy and stay out of the hospital.

"Bunny rabbits, birds, bees.… Frosty the snowman.…"

This story was originally a gift from a husband to his loving wife for Christmas. The wife is the mother of a special needs child. It was…It is…the best gift *I* (the author) could think of.

VISION

I stood at the back of the long line with my head tilted to one side and I peered toward the front, trying to estimate how long it would take before I'd finally get a drink. If it had been the night before, out with my buddies at the local pub after a Friday night softball game, I'd simply offer a few soft elbows, use my size and maneuver my way to the bar to request immediate service. However, tonight's more elegant surroundings dictated a different course of conduct.

After a good ten minutes of being patient, biting my tongue, and slowly ebbing my way forward, I finally found himself at the front of the drink line. But, before I could even place my drink order, an old man suddenly came out of nowhere and cut right in front of me.

"What different options do you have to drink?" the old man who had but-in asked the bartender. The old man acted nonchalant and seemed completely oblivious to all the people standing in the long line. The bartender, meanwhile, didn't even hesitate, and began reciting the long list of cocktail options, which included the different brands of beers and wines in stock clearly visible on a shelf behind the bar. The old man then proceeded to slowly order three different drinks, all of which were complicated tropical concoctions, the kind with tiny umbrellas. I rolled my eyes at this point and flinched with growing impatience. I grimaced as if ready to say or do something drastic, but then I caught myself and thought better of it. Instead, I took a deep breath and chose a different tact. I decided to offer some assistance to the old man, albeit with sarcasm.

"Excuse me, sir," I said, as I leaned forward a bit. "Do you need any help carrying all those drinks back to your table?" The old man turned to face me and politely declined assistance. It was at that point clear to everyone in the line that the old man was, in fact, blind. The old man, instead, requested a small tray from the bartender, which could be used to carry the drinks in his "empty" hand opposite his retractable walking stick, which everyone thought was a cane. I chewed on my thoughts while marveling at the old man's ability to manage without anyone's help and then walk across the room, through traffic, and delivering the drinks without incident to his table. The physical gift of sight is something not always appreciated by people who can see. Watching a blind person do ordinary, everyday tasks right in front of you can be both educational and impressive. "Oh, and by the way," the old man added right before he left the bar area, "forgive me, everyone, for butting in line. I had no idea."

"Where have you been?" asked my wife when I finally returned with our drinks to where she was standing in the silent auction gallery room. The tone in her voice displayed a slight disapproval with my delay, mostly because she knew my penchant for taking longer then I should on trips to the bar, often stopping to talk to people for extended periods and, therefore, leaving her often all by herself. As she awaited a typical, non-culpable response, she continued gazing at the student-prepared art exhibits on a nearby table, items which were up for bid.

Instead of answering my wife's question directly, I decided to move things along and I, too, started to examine the paintings displayed on the tables. Eventually, I remarked, "Wow! These paintings are really quite impressive. The fact that they were all done by blind students is almost unbelievable." My wife and I were two of the four hundred guests in attendance for the big fundraising event, which celebrated the long proud history of the Main Line School for the Blind. The cocktail party, silent auction, and black-tie dinner to follow in the grand ballroom was at the prestigious Hyatt Hotel, which overlooked the Delaware River on Penn's Landing in Center City, Philadelphia, and commemorated the school's proud 175-year history of serving individuals with visual impairments. We had a multi-handicapped, blind, twelve-year-old daughter who attended the school. We were just two of the many parents in attendance.

My wife gently nudged my arm at that point and said softly, "Here comes Grace's teacher."

A young woman approached, smiling as she extended a warm, cordial greeting. Her name was Gretchen Duffy. After a few casual exchanges about the beautiful setting for the affair and the wonderful purpose for the occasion, young Ms. Duffy offered some specific updates regarding our Grace who had been Gretchen's student for several years. After providing a thorough synopsis of recent school activities, class trips, and Grace's significant continued progress with the occupational therapy program, the teacher added some extra insight. "Grace is my little angel, you know," Ms. Duffy said plainly. "Not just because she looks like an angel with her blond curly hair, blue eyes, and porcelain white skin, mind you; but, Grace inspires me and many others a great deal every day. I'm always talking about her to my boyfriend." The teacher paused and started to sort through her purse, eventually pulling out a picture she had of Grace. "In fact, last year, I even had a dream that Grace appeared in. The dream convinced me to go back to school for my masters in special education, which in fact, I'm pursuing right now. Grace is a gift to all her teachers, the administration, and the aides."

My wife and I listened intently to the kind words and were in no way surprised with the attributions. We believed that our daughter Grace had a magical, spiritual quality about her and we had stopped questioning the stories, occurrences, and coincidences. While her disabilities were multiple, complex and severe, Grace had certain abilities that defied all logic…almost like a musical savant, someone who might be a severe mentally retarded individual, but could somehow play the piano like a concert-level classical pianist. For example, Grace, who could not see according to all the tests and the doctors, would immediately call out our names any time we quietly snuck up in front of her. Also, she had completely memorized over 100 different people simply by the sound of their voices, pretty impressive, most agreed, for a severely mentally-handicapped child who couldn't add three plus two.

∽∾

My wife and I mingled during the cocktail hour, observed the student artwork on display, and perused the silent auction items. I considered myself, among other things, an amateur restaurant critic and a self-proclaimed sports fanatic; so, I placed various bids on restaurant gift certificates and the sports tickets available. As we made our way through the crowds, we happened to draw close to a gentleman I had recently met at a business chamber of commerce function. The man was Pennsylvania State Senator Daniel McFadden. "Danny," as he was known to his friends and supporters, was a powerful force in the state capital of Harrisburg, and known to be an advocate for individuals with special needs. His rise to power among the political ranks had stirred great excitement and hope throughout the special needs communities. With Danny where he was now, there was legitimate hope for changes in the laws to improve the bureaucratic red tape, thereby providing additional funding and programs for special needs education.

So, I tried to catch the senator's attention by trying to make eye contact and when I did, I extended my hand. "Good evening, Senator," I said.

The senator looked back with a friendly smile, seemed to recognize me and we exchanged formal introductions. My wife and I then ensued to have a charming and quite lengthy conversation with the senator, who seemed genuinely interested to hear all about our daughter Grace and our family's strong appreciation for the Main Line School for the Blind. We told the senator about some of our daughter's unique abilities, her penchant for inspiring people, and also about the magical event which occurred to Grace a few years back when we traveled to Rome. The senator seemed fascinated to hear about Grace and spent a good twenty minutes talking with us. I felt guilty. At one point, I even asked the senator if we were keeping him from mingling with others. The senator insisted he was content where he was and wanted to hear the stories about Grace.

After chatting at length with the senator, we eventually made our way to the far corner of the room to watch the DVD video, which contained a history about the school and had dozens of converted old photographs which spanned generations. The video detailed the school's original mission, the current day goals, talked about the impressive physical facilities, and provided mini-biographies about some of the most famous alumni.

∽∾∾

At the conclusion of the cocktail hour, the call for dinner came and we followed the masses into the vast ballroom where we found our seats at one of the tables reserved for parents of students. Once seated, I started a conversation with the woman immediately to my right, trying my best to talk over the splendid music coming from the twelve-piece orchestra up on the stage. The themes for the music selections played included Broadway musicals and songs from the Big Band era. The Hyatt ballroom decor was exquisite for the occasion.

The woman seated next to me, meanwhile, went on at length about her eight year-old blind son who also had cerebral palsy. She spoke openly about the drastic demise of her marriage resulting from all the stress related to her son's health and handicaps. Her husband apparently couldn't handle it and one day just got up and left. He blamed her. He said she'd become too obsessed with caring for their disabled son, that their marriage couldn't make it. Now the single mother of a special needs child, she explained how she dedicated her entire life to her son.

"The thing that helped me the most, though," the woman said, "was the support group at the school for parents of multi-handicapped children. The administration personnel put me in touch with the group and I started going to the meetings. It helped a lot being around people dealing with the same type of issues. Before, I felt so alone. Now, I have a much healthier outlook and overall perspective."

I simply nodded. Normally, I might have shared some of the trials and tribulations that my own family and our Grace had gone through, such as the forty-six or so hospitalizations up to that point, Grace's four major surgeries, and the seventeen doses of medicine Grace took every single day for all her different conditions; but, I figured this was one of those occasions where I just needed to listen.

∽∾

At the conclusion of the delicious dinner, while coffee and dessert were being served, the master of ceremony for the affair, a well-known local TV sports-caster, walked up to the podium. He broke the ice by telling a few sports-re-lated jokes and then introduced the school's Board of Directors, the school principal, and some of the longest tenured teachers in attendance. The emcee then proceeded to begin with presenting the Distinguished Honoree Award. At this point, I picked up a program and flipped to the page to read about the intended honoree. The recipient of the award was slated to be none other than Senator McFadden.

"When I think of Danny McFadden," the emcee began, "I think of a great quarterback, who can see the entire field and can thread the needle to his intended receiver for a game-winning touchdown, or a superstar basketball player racing down the floor on a fast break and able to find an open teammate for an easy bas-ket with only seconds left on the clock, or a gritty hockey player with a sixth sense who can somehow pass the puck behind his back between a defenseman's skates to a line mate for a big goal. Danny has these types of innate, God-given skills and the same kind of leadership qualities. He works well with his legislative team-mates and he tries his best to get things done." The audience sat back in a relaxed silent mode, listening to the analogies along with the well-deserved accolades.

"But more important than these special qualities," the emcee went on, "Senator Danny McFadden genuinely cares about people and especially individuals with special needs. He's a friend in the state capitol for all those with disabilities. Ladies and gentlemen, it is my distinct pleasure tonight to introduce my dear friend, Senator Daniel McFadden." The emcee then stepped off to the side of the podium and the crowd provided a boisterous applause, which was deserved, and gave the whole affair an added festive quality.

Senator McFadden made his way from his table and walked up to the podium. He had white index cards in one hand while he waved to the crowd with his other. His warm, appreciative smile beamed and he appeared quite touched by the honor.

Considered a polished speaker according to all sources, the senator quickly gathered himself at the podium and perused the room. The applause slowly lessened. As quiet returned to the ballroom, he looked down at the index cards in his hands and began to speak.

"I had a short speech prepared for tonight," he started out as he raised and then lowered the white cards to the podium. "But, instead of the intended speech I wrote, I'd like to tell everyone a story. It's a story I heard just tonight for the first time and a story that moved me a great deal." The senator looked around the vast room and then focused his attentions on the parent tables to the far side of the room.

"Two proud parents told me tonight about their daughter, who is one of the many students at the Main Line School for the Blind." As the senator spoke his chosen words, my wife looked toward me with a bewildered look. She instantly became emotional. The other parents at the table all expressed puzzled looks toward us.

Senator McFadden went on, "Does everyone here know that little Grace Bowen went to Rome a few years back with the Archdiocese of Philadelphia for the Millennium Jubilee Mass for the Disabled?" The senator paused as the words hung in the huge ballroom air. "And on that special day, little Grace was a six-year-old ambassador of sorts from our fair city. And somehow, miraculously, on that fateful day, she was picked at random out of crowd of thousands and handed to the Pope. She was then hugged, kissed, and blessed by his eminence, Pope John Paul II!" Tears welled up in the eyes of my wife. Meanwhile, I fought back a wave of raw emotion myself. The story was our daughter's big day...perhaps what will be the biggest day she will ever have in her entire life. The senator continued.

"Grace's parents told me tonight during the cocktail hour about how their daughter, *because* of her handicaps...how she inspires people. They told me that it is Grace who teaches *them* about life and how to put things in perspective. It is little Grace who shows by example how to handle adversity in life and how to love absolutely and unconditionally. It, therefore, occurred to me tonight, ladies and gentlemen, that you, the *parents* out there in the audience and you, the *administrators, aides,* and *teachers* at the Main Line School for the Blind… *you folks* are the ones who really deserve an award. You are the ones every day helping, loving, and taking care of handicapped children like Grace, encouraging them to be the best they can be, given severe obstacles and tremendous challenges. Therefore, it is *my privilege* to be your honoree tonight. I simply and humbly say thank you."

As the senator concluded his remarks, the crowd of four hundred strong in the ballroom rose to their feet and gave a thunderous standing ovation, which continued for several minutes. It went unsaid, but many were applauding much more than the honoree, himself. It was the senator's words that brought out the poignant and insightful points. People smiled from ear to ear while they clapped and many had tears in their eyes. It was quite a spectacle to behold.

✵

Question for the reader:

1. How many different types of "vision" are revealed in the story? To answer this question, the reader is directed to look up the definition of the word "vision" in the dictionary.

TRUE COMMUNION

As the glass doors opened into the glistening sunlight, Grace made her way outside onto the slate patio, doing her best not to fall as she walked. The nurse and Grace's Aunt Casey both walked slowly beside her, each holding one of Grace's delicate little hands. Grace's mother followed behind them, smiling proudly and pushing the wheelchair-stroller filled with supplies. Grace's father, with only his head visible to the crowd, brought up the rear, his arms full of presents. The plan was for Grace to make a dramatic entrance to the party, mostly of her own volition, thereby showing off both her improved walking abilities and the pristine white-silk beautiful Communion dress her "Gamma" had bought for her.

As Grace continued across the patio, her short, curly blonde hair feathered in the early May breeze. The refreshing, mild winds flowed in off the plush green fairways of the golf course and gave all those under the canopy a welcome relief from the unseasonably warm spring weather. No complainers, though, in the group one would surmise, not after a six-snowstorm, extremely cold, Bucks County, Pennsylvania, winter and what seemed like a solid month thereafter of rain. Flowers blossomed everywhere now. Beautiful purple and pink New Guinea impatiens and an array of colored tulips lined the country club walkways and the beds on the patio perimeter. The vibrant assortment of flowers established proof of the official arrival of spring and also provided the perfect visual backdrop for Grace's angelic ensemble. From a distance, under this combination of almost perfect conditions, one would hardly know she was a severe mentally and physically handicapped child with a myriad of debilitating medical conditions.

"Grace is here," proclaimed Shannon, the younger sister and co-star of the day. She had arrived a few minutes earlier, having begged to drive with Gamma for the short ride from the church. Shannon stood up quickly and with clear purpose. She wore an identical dress. Standing, Shannon's natural beauty was captivating, something clearly to behold. She had matching blue eyes and thick long blonde hair, which cascaded down to the small of her back. Shannon immediately headed over to greet her special sister.

With Shannon coming toward them, the nurse and Aunt Casey simultaneously let go of Grace's hands and watched the sibling encounter ensue. Grace, in her typical awkward-yet-determined fashion, gave her best effort to walk toward the noises of the crowd, where she was met halfway by Shannon in loving fashion. The group of fifty or so family members and friends in attendance, either seated or standing at the outside portable bar, watched in sheer delight as the pair of first Holy Communion recipients hugged each other for an extended period. Their father and mother stood close-by on the sides, just in case Grace, God forbid, lost her balance and fell. Usually, when walking, and because she was considered legally blind, Grace wore a bike helmet of sorts to protect her head from a possible tumble, but not on this day, they had decided…such an important occasion and with such a beautiful outfit on display.

The idea for the double Communion party had come about a few months back after the parish pastor and the CCD/religious education coordinator for Shannon advised they would all work together with Grace's special-education teachers to prepare her in time to receive the sacrament along with her younger sister. Grace, though fourteen months the elder, was physically the smaller of the two; but when standing together they looked much like twins. And today, they were truly sharing the identical limelight. The unique Holy Communion Mass, celebrated earlier that morning in their parish, had turned out to be both a beautiful ceremony for all the regular second-graders in the parish and a touching testament for including the disabled in parish events, when special arrangements were made for Grace to receive the Eucharist for the first time.

The entire congregation looked on patiently and with tempered concern as the pastor, the nurse, and Grace's mother made numerous collective efforts to get Grace to finally accept a tiny sliver of the Body of Christ, helped along by a spoon and small Dixie cup of water. Many profoundly disabled oftentimes are orally defensive when it comes to placing anything close to their mouths and Grace was worse than most. The difficulties with such a seemingly simple task gave the captured audience a brief glimpse into the world of a very involved special needs child. The poignancy of the moment was then magnified tenfold when, all-on-her-own, Grace blurted out loudly "Amen" at the appropriate time. The weeks of repetitive, loving training by Grace's devoted teachers and her parents had made the mark, as if somehow inspired or assisted by divine intervention.

∽∾∾

"It's time for Grace's medicine," said her mother, speaking to everyone in the group who knew what that directive entailed and so that the necessary roles would be assumed. The process began with dad pulling Grace gently toward him and holding her as he sat back on a folding chair. Grace instinctively edged herself happily onto his lap. The nurse then opened the large carry-bag of supplies and drew out the pre-measured syringe with the designated labeled anti-seizure medicine. Grace's mother started to garner control of Grace's hands so she wouldn't flail her arms or throw her head—her distinct way of contesting the rather considerable noontime dosage. Receiving medicine was not Grace's favorite thing to do and who could blame her, with a total of seventeen doses of assorted medicines each and every day. In fact, the recent change in the anti-convulsant medication recommended by the neurologist and deemed necessary because of the increasing hyperactivity caused by the former medicine, created a heightened concern for another febrile seizure during this the adjustment period. On several occasions over the years when a seizure had followed a sudden spike in temperature, Grace had actually stopped breathing, which is why the family traveled everywhere with a portable oxygen tank and mask with them. The CPR emergency equipment was tucked in the basket underneath the stroller and next to the fully-charged cell phone. So, understandably, everyone was on constant high alert for the usual symptoms, which often came without much warning.

The biggest worry, though, according to the doctors, was another serious bladder infection and more permanent kidney scarring. Of Grace's fifteen doctors, the nephrologist was the one that scared them the most with the possible, down-the-road scenarios because of Grace's already severely scarred and limited functioning kidneys.

"Okay, let's everyone sing a nursery rhyme to Grace," said her dad, referring to the distraction tactic employed most often to prevent Grace from a self-induced behavioral gagging episode. The gagging could result in the spitting up of the much-needed medicine. "Let's go with *Twinkle, Twinkle Little Star*," he said. "It's one of her favorites."

"And here, Daddy," said Shannon, while reaching toward a nearby table and grabbing a large linen napkin. "I got you a towel, just in case." She was trying to help, as usual; matured by past experiences beyond her years. The musical efforts of the group did the trick and nearly stayed in sync with the songbirds chirping high in the trees above the nearby putting green.

While applying the towel to prevent a spill on Grace's beautiful white dress, Grace's dad was also very careful not to get anything caught up with the rosary beads in his own hands, which he brought with him for the day. The special rosary beads belonged to Grace and were an everyday reminder of the biggest day in Grace's life when she was selected out of a crowd of thousands at the Millennium Jubilee Mass for the handicapped in Rome, Italy, and handed to Pope John Paul II. The procession for the Pope that day was, in fact, halted for Grace to be carried to him. The Holy Father took Grace up into his arms, kissed her, hugged her, blessed her and then handed her back to her father. The rosary beads had been tucked underneath Grace's dress when the blessing occurred, secured in a travel money belt.

"Can we do anything to help?" asked Aunt Casey, as she walked over. She was referring to herself and the three other paternal aunts, all standing around looking ready to assist.

"Yeah," said Grace and Shannon's dad, with a half-serious tone. "You can get me a cold beer for one thing and then tell everyone else to have a seat, lunch will be served in a few minutes." He laughed somewhat as everyone took his light-hearted cue and then he added, "Oh, and tell Great Aunt Gertrude no more whiskey sours…we're cutting her off."

✄

"Mary Beth, will you get the stroller for me?" asked Grace's mother, speaking to the nurse after the medicine was administered. "I think Grace is getting tired from all the excitement and stimulation; she needs to sit quietly for a while. We don't want her to have another seizure again from too much excitement. And, I also think we'd better change her diaper one more time before lunch gets started." They worked together swiftly to make sure Grace drank more water to keep with her necessary daily fluids schedule, so important because of her faulty kidneys. Everything Grace drank and ate each day had to be recorded in order to stay on top of her infirmities and to try and prevent problems.

Behind everyone on a long white table, placed next to the mountain of neatly wrapped presents, was the huge first Holy Communion sheet cake—four square feet of pure butter cream fantasia with bright pink icing swirled in large, fancy writing. The cake revealed the two girls' names and bespoke the special occasion. At the bottom of the cake was smaller writing, insisted upon by their father at the bakery, which read: THE ANGEL AND THE ACTRESS.

❧

"Let's say a prayer before the meal," said Uncle Jimmy after everyone was seated. He had prepared something special for the occasion of his nieces' special day, as he often was apt to do for family events. His brief but reflective words reminded everyone of the importance of good health in life and the benefit of perspective when contemplating life's many problems.

"What a menu!" asserted family friend, Glen Duffy, the moment the prayer was concluded. He was a weekend chef of sorts, a fan of the Food Channel shows on cable TV and one of the close family friends invited to the celebration. Glen's comment was for everyone at the tables to hear, but directed primarily toward Ben and Sara, an older couple who were also 'extended' family members. Sara and Ben were culinary aficionados, as well, with Sara also being the designated official photographer for the day. "The appetizer," Glen went on, describing the menu, "is called Shrimp Legion, which I never even heard of before, but it looks totally awesome and there are three different options for the entrée: Poached North Atlantic Salmon, Chicken Angelica with Pasta, and Grilled Filet Mignon. No offense to Grace's puréed sweet potatoes over there, but I'm in culinary heaven here.... Bam!"

"Okay, everyone," said the emphatically happy father with an added emphasis, trying to draw the group's attention as he stood up for purposes of a toast. He focused on his two beautiful daughters, glowing in their white communion dresses. He cleared his throat as he scanned the fifty or so happy faces around the tables and then pointedly said, "I'd just like to say two simple words... Let's eat!"

❧

Question for the reader:

1. On how many levels do you see a "communion" in the story?

Easter at Gamma's

Easter is my favorite day of the year…without a doubt. Sitting in my designated, extra-comfortable chair at my Gamma's house, waiting for dinner to be served; I can't help but look around and be happy. My Gamma always works so hard to prepare the house and all the food for our annual visit. She makes everything so special. That's why I call her, "Sweetie Pie."

This morning, for instance, we had so much fun. My mother woke me up and, while still in our pajamas, the whole family went into the den to see what the Easter Bunny had left for us. Gamma had the camera and couldn't take enough pictures. Together, we checked in front of the fireplace to see whether the big bunny had eaten the carrot my sissy and I had left for him. The Easter Bunny had chomped half the carrot, leaving the rest on the plate. On the red bricks in front of the fireplace, there were two big wicker Easter baskets for my sissy and me, with our names taped on them. My sister's basket was loaded with green-colored plastic grass, big chocolate bunnies, jelly beans, and chocolate eggs of all sizes. Now, since I don't eat candy, my basket was filled with different stuff—all of my favorite things, though, such as beautiful colored ribbons, storybooks, music tapes, and a big soft white stuffed bunny rabbit. I'm always amazed how the Easter Bunny knows exactly what to bring me and makes a special basket each year just for me. My younger sister Shannon couldn't contain herself, of course, and she started eating some of the candy right away. My mother told her to stop and save the candy till later. My sister gets very excited with these type things, which is understandable, since she's only ten.

After breakfast, we all put on our coats and shoes and then went outside for an Easter egg hunt in the backyard. Pebbles, our little Yorkie Terrier, burst out the back door first and led our team with the adventure. She scurried all over the yard, sniffing and trying her best to find the eggs. Mostly, though, she barked at the birds up in the trees. I noticed as we got outside how spring had arrived. It was a warm, sunny morning. The sun felt good on my face. The grass was so green. Tulips and daffodils were blooming in the flower beds and birds were singing everywhere, both in the trees and in the many birdfeeders my Gamma had hanging all over the yard. My mother held my hand and walked with me as we found some plastic eggs in their hiding places. Some were under bushes, some next to flowers, and others on the backyard picnic table seats. The eggs weren't too hard to find, if you asked me.

"Oh, I see one!" blurted out my Great Aunt Gertrude, as she pointed at the ground over near the wood pile, then started walking in that direction.

My mother quickly replied, "The eggs are for the children, Aunt Gertrude." My mother then led me over and I added another plastic egg to my collection. We had little bags to collect the plastic eggs, which each had candy inside. My sissy ended up with the most eggs.

The night before, after we'd finished coloring the cooked Easter eggs at the kitchen table, my father announced that we were all going to watch the movie *Jesus of Nazareth*, which is his requirement every year on Holy Saturday night. He calls it the "single best movie ever made about Jesus Christ." I agree, even though its four hours long and I've never seen the whole movie at one given time. I never make it more than an hour or so before I fall asleep or it's my bedtime. I love watching the movie, though, especially sitting on my father's lap and hugging him. My dad usually stays up late and watches the conclusion by himself.

My bedtime routine is quite involved, so it takes a while for me to get ready. First, I get a bath and a diaper change. After that, it's into my pajamas. Then, I have to take all my nighttime medicines, which my mother gives me slowly, using pre-measured syringes. I get a lot of medicine every day to prevent seizures and stuff. After all the medicine, my mother gives me water to drink, which she needs to do constantly because of my kidney problems. Of course, a lot of water right before bed quickly leads to a wet diaper soon enough. That's why my mother always gets up in the middle of the night at least once to change my diaper. Being an eleven-year-old child with disabilities is busy business.

∽

The day before, on the way driving to Gamma's on Holy Saturday morning, my father told us the story about the origins of the Easter Bunny in the United States. The ride to Gamma's, outside of Princeton, New Jersey, coming from our house in Bucks County, Pennsylvania, usually takes about an hour or so and always seems a lot shorter when my father tells his stories. Some stories are real and others, I think, he makes up.

Anyway, as we drove here yesterday, my father told the Easter Bunny story and talked the whole time like he was a TV sports announcer. He explained to us that the Easter Bunny came to America initially from Germany, along with the Pennsylvania Dutch in the 1700s. The giant bunny allegedly snuck on-board a huge cargo ship, which was bringing food and supplies to the New World. Legend has it, that the giant bunny was hiding the whole time in a large wooden shipment full of eggs. The giant bunny was so happy when he finally made it to America safely that he swore to bring colored eggs to all the children around the country on a special day every year. He picked Easter. My father paused at that point, smiled at my mother in the front passenger seat, then continued. "You see, kids, years ago Catholics were not allowed to eat eggs during Lent, they were forbidden as part of fasting; so on Easter, many people celebrated by eating lots of eggs. Eggs are actually very symbolic."

At this particular juncture I tried to contribute to the conversation. I spoke up from the backseat of the car and said a few things, but my words came out scattered, bumbled, and random. My inner thoughts are one thing, but, unfortunately, when I try to verbalize, I often have trouble. I got out "bunny rabbits" and "Easter Bunny." I said those words again a few more times.

∽◡∾

We all went to ten o'clock Mass earlier today. My sister and I were dressed in our matching yellow Easter dresses with fluffy white bonnets. I kept pulling the bonnet off my head, though, because I hate hats. My Gamma loves when we all go to church together, especially her church. She absolutely beams when we walk in and out of the church together. We usually stop and talk to her Pastor after Mass. A lot of times, the ushers even ask us to take up the gifts, which I personally love to do. I love going to church. I love all the music and the singing. I love to clap my hands and I try my best to sing along. I have to give Gamma credit, too, because with all my problems walking and talking, a lot of people often look at me funny and that can be kind of awkward. Sometimes, I even need to wear metal braces on my legs to help me walk. My dad kids me when I do and says I look like Forrest Gump, just much, much prettier. And my Gamma, well, she couldn't be prouder of me.

Speaking of my Gamma, you should see the way she gets her house ready for our annual Easter visit. My father jokes that Gamma starts getting ready the day after we leave the year before. The house is clean as a whistle, with everything organized meticulously. Everything is set up for all my special needs. My food has to be pureed, so Gamma and my mother work together to have that all done in advance and labeled in the refrigerator. A diaper-changing station is set in place for me in the extra bedroom, with enough supplies for a nuclear fallout. I don't know what that term means exactly, but I heard my father make the reference several times. Also, Gamma has a big box in the living room filled with all my favorite things—strings and ribbons, nursery rhyme books, music tapes, and stuffed animals—all for me to play with. I love twirling strings and ribbons in my hands. She also has cassette tape players in almost every room in the house because she knows how much I like music and how it soothes me when I get hyper. She even has extra batteries next to the cassette players, just in case. Since Easter is the only time I get to go to Gamma's house each year, I savor it. I absolutely love every single minute when I'm there. I'm named after my Gamma, you know—my middle name is Margaret.

∽∾∾

This year, my Uncle Jimmy organized a treasure hunt game, which we played after Mass. He told us, "The winner gets a treasure chest, full of coins." He left paper clues all over the house. The clues were taped to stuff like the mirror, the microwave, and the clock. Each clue led you to the next place, if you figured it out. We all did the treasure hunt together and we had a lot of fun going from room to room. At the end, my sissy and I both won a dollar's worth of quarters, which were stuffed in little jewelry boxes. We found the little treasure chests inside my Gamma's boots. The old rain boots were in the front closet. The little jewelry boxes had our names written on them and each marked with a big 'X.' We felt like pirates.

One thing struck me while we were scavenging throughout the house looking for treasure. I remembered what had happened the year before on Easter, when I had suffered a really bad seizure while taking a walk in the neighborhood with everyone. I don't remember the actual seizure, just what everyone said about it afterward. Apparently, I started having real scary convulsions, like I do sometimes when my medicine levels are low or I get a high fever. My father carried me back to Gamma's house and my mother had to give me a Diastat suppository in order to bring me out of the seizure. They also administered oxygen from the portable oxygen tank my mother carries with her all the time. She carries it with her everywhere, ever since the one incident years' back, when I stopped breathing completely, while they were waiting for the paramedics to arrive. Fortunately, I came out of the seizure quickly last Easter and they didn't even have to call 911 again.

∽∾

We usually eat our Easter dinner at three o'clock in the afternoon, so we don't have to rush home right after dinner and also so that we're finished in time for my father to watch the end of the big golf tournament sometimes on TV. My father calls our Easter dinner a Polish feast straight from Wadowice, Poland, which is the town where Pope John Paul II was born. My father is a big fan of Pope John Paul II for many reasons and especially because I met him once. My dad says the Pope and I are friends. All I know is he kissed me, hugged me, and blessed me.

Anyway, my Gamma purchases most of the food for our Easter dinner at a Polish deli and bakery located in Manville, New Jersey. She says she has to stand in a long line in order to get everything she needs, but she doesn't mind. Manville is a very Polish community about ten minutes away from her house. My Gamma loves cooking. She always serves pierogies, kielbasa, borscht soup with horseradish shavings on top, baked ham, homemade potato salad, babka, and chrystiki. I eat pierogies, but my food has to be mashed up and pureed.

Every year, my father insists on saying grace before our Easter dinner, which is okay with me, especially since my name is Grace and I love to pray. Usually, my father says a short prayer, giving thanks to God for everything we have, and then he reads the definition of Easter straight from the dictionary. Each year he tells us, "Easter is the feast that commemorates Christ's resurrection and is observed with variations of dates due to different calendars on the first Sunday after the paschal full moon." I think that sounds pretty neat, even though I don't know what it all means.

∽∾

Last year we even stayed extra late because we all wanted to watch *The Sound of Music* on TV. My Gamma loves that movie. We all do. I guess you could say it's our favorite movie to watch together as a family. We finally left Gamma's last year around nine o'clock at night, which was way past my bedtime. And when we were backing the car down the driveway, my Gamma stood in the garage doorway crying. I cried, too, in the backseat of our car.

∽◦∾

So, as I sit here now watching my Gamma running in and out of the kitchen and placing all the delicious food on the dining room table, I want to appreciate the Easter holiday as much as possible and, also, I hope my Gamma lives for-ever. I wonder sometimes what might change from one year to the next.

I wish Easter could be every day of the year.

LIFE IS A PICNIC

Forty hospital admissions and four surgeries in ten years.... Wow! I said out loud, as I stared out the car windshield at the open highway in front of me. As I drove along by myself, I contemplated those rather significant numbers, along with the insightful words of our parish priest, Father McDevitt, from the Sunday homily earlier that morning. The priest's mention of the "crosses of life" at the 7:30 Mass had been a bit ironic to me and started a familiar chain reaction of thoughts, which usually resulted in more questions than answers. The topic had so many modern day meanings and connotations, yet, all the proverbial roads eventually led back by literal and scriptural reference to the Crucifixion of Jesus Christ.

Keeping my eyes on the road, I sorted in my head the difficult trials and tribulations of the last week where our oldest daughter Grace had, once again, been admitted in an emergency situation to the big children's hospital downtown. The series of events had been brutal overall and her doctors were still unclear whether she was getting better or worse on the latest "new" antibiotic. The blur of everything was mentally exhausting.

Each day of the hospital admission, my wife sat at our daughter's bedside and helped the nurses with the necessary care for Grace, which was quite involved, in fact, overwhelming. The daily care routine started with the schedule for the seventeen regular doses of medicine she received each day as a norm; then, there was the additional antibiotic medicine for the pneumonia. In addition, Grace needed diaper changes every two hours and then there was the complicated, painful world of maintaining a functioning IV for fluids and nutrition; the IV task being the hardest, since Grace's veins were small and severely scarred from all the prior hospital admissions. To make matters even more difficult, Grace constantly tried to rip the invasive IVs out of her body whenever she could. As a result, she had to wear soft elbow protective braces called "No-Nos," in the hospital so that she couldn't bend her arms to reach the IV lines, monitors, and tubes. Then they taped socks on her hands so she couldn't take off the "No-Nos." If she did somehow break through all the obstructions and rip out another IV, the medical team would then have to start all over again. Each time they gave her a fresh IV, little Grace kicked, screamed, and cried.

Each night during the week, I completed the care routine circle. After working a full day at my law office, I would routinely drive downtown and relieve my wife for the night shift, which generally meant sleeping next to Grace on a pull-out hospital chair-couch. Someone had to be in the room with Grace at all times because of her unique combination of disabilities and abilities. She couldn't be left alone for a single second. On one hand, she was physically and mentally severely handicapped and legally blind. On the other hand, our little angel from God could walk, which was a good thing by itself, but also meant she could try to leave at any time, or at the very least fall out of the hospital bed, if left unattended.

The most recent five-day stint in the intensive care unit downtown had taken a particularly significant toll both on Grace's frail little body and our family's constitution, as the Thanksgiving holiday approached. The most recent medical misadventure involved a new problem to add to the long list— severe pneumonia with lung scarring a likely result. The now re-occurring pneumonia condition raised all kinds of additional problems to Grace's already difficult and complicated medical scenario. Now, whenever Grace spiked a fever, there were at least "nine" different possible underlying causes for Mom, Dad, the doctors, and the nurses to quickly decipher before she had another seizure. The customary rush to the nearest hospital because of a high fever, before a scary febrile seizure entered the equation, was a standard occurrence, as was the constant monitoring and maintaining enough fluids each day because her kidneys didn't work well.

The local hospital emergency room standard procedure was to employ an extensive litany of tests and exams in order to determine the underlying root of the fever. The tests and exams often did more harm than good to little Grace. Sometimes, the underlying cause was nothing more than a simple cold, a virus, or an ordinary flu; but, still, all the tests were necessary in order to rule out the more serious possibilities, such as a bad ear infection, a shunt malfunction, more kidney trouble, another bowel obstruction, or another dreaded urinary tract infection. One of the problems also was that Grace had been administered so many antibiotics over the years, she was now immune to some of them, therefore, they no longer worked. On top of all that, we now had pneumonia to consider. My wife and I prayed vigilantly during all the hospitalizations that our little special needs daughter didn't go into septic shock again—that was a real nightmare, the time that happened.

The other aspect weighing on my mind, as I drove southbound on I-95 headed toward Center City Philadelphia and, subconsciously, observing the impressive skyscrapers off in the distance, was the hope that Grace would be out of the hospital in time for Thanksgiving, which was now only a few short days away. She had spent so many holidays in the hospital over the years, I'd stopped counting that particular figure. However, when she was healthy and home for a particular holiday, that simple fact alone was appreciated so dearly by everyone in the family, and all by itself, made the holiday a wonderful celebration.

Some people might call it perspective. We had learned to note the marked contrasts in life and enjoy the happy moments when we could. A severely handicapped, special needs child with a lot of medical problems can help you do that.

∽∾

Grace loved picnics. She loved everything about picnics. She even loved saying the word "picnic." Because of that, our family had a lot of family picnics. Perhaps, the causal connection was in reality, actually set in reverse, but either way, friends and family came to know that Sunday was the designated family day in our household for a picnic. The goal each week, weather permitting, was either a picnic at Grace's school or a backyard gathering with all the trimmings, which meant the portable TV with the bunny ears antenna, the electric line, the wooden outdoor TV stand, comfortable fluffy lawn blankets, beach chairs, a hammock set up between the trees, the beverage cooler, a big picnic basket, and most important of all…the Wiffle ball bat and ball. This way, our family could watch the city's home team play a baseball or football game, while lounging in the sunshine or sitting under the shade of the backyard trees; all the time with fresh air filling our lungs and feeling almost as if we were down at the ballpark. Meanwhile, if our little Grace needed medicine, a nap, a diaper change, or if any health complications arose, we weren't in a compromising situation at a foreign unmanageable location. Instead, we could simply go inside our house and take care of business.

The basic concept of trudging everything a mere distance of only thirty feet from the garage into our very own backyard constituted the genius component of the equation and also provided the aura of returning to the fabric of a simpler generation from days gone by. The neighbors sometimes looked at us a little funny, but heck, what did they know? Of course, the truest point probably would be that we had simply adapted to what life had given us and we were trying to do our best under the circumstances. Some people may think it would be more enjoyable to take the whole family to the actual ballpark, but not for us.

∽

Grace loved to talk and she talked constantly. She often talked in a scattering of repeated, unassociated words, often seemingly at random, but sometimes with an absolute sense of knowing the situation and her surroundings. At times, she was a complete chatterbox and she especially liked to talk at length about her younger sister, Shannon aka "Sissy." Sissy this…Sissy that.… It was amazing just to sit, watch, and listen to Grace. For example, while sitting or standing, Grace would call out the name of a person the minute she heard his or her voice, somehow knowing who it was, even though she was legally blind and the person speaking was, say, standing twenty or so feet behind her. For another example, she learned to whisper whenever she entered a church, which was sweet and fascinating to observe. She had a very spiritual quality about her and somehow a sense about her surroundings. Further, when Grace listened to one of her many music or nursery rhymes tapes, she often memorized the beat and the words quicker than others around her, those without any learning disabilities or impairments. She sweetly sang along with the words of the songs. In a way, she was a savant when it came to music and sounds. It was hard to know just how much she comprehended and how much she truly understood. She was captivating to listen to and decipher, especially since she couldn't add two numbers if you asked her to do a simple math problem. She was entertaining and even utilized by her friends and family as a weapon for fun. She could be engaged to say something clever about another person coming into the room. It was all done by memorization and word association. For example, Great Aunt Gertrude is a "pain in the neck," being one of the favorite on cue remarks when asked. As Grace got older, she learned to ask for what she wanted, such as when she grew sleepy at night, she'd often turn to her mother and softly say, "Time for bed."

A big part of the overall magic of Grace, especially in light of her severe disabilities and extensive health problems, was her angelic appearance, which seemed almost eerie under the circumstances. Here she was, a severe, mentally profound, multiple-physically handicapped child; and her name was Grace and she was born on All Saints' Day, November 1, 1994. Then, believe it or not, when someone opened a book about angels, she looked exactly like the actual angel Grace as depicted in the angel books. Grace was a beautiful child, appearing like a cherub, as if touched directly by the hand of God with some greater purpose in mind. She had curly blond hair, sparkling blue eyes, porcelain white skin, rosy red cheeks, and tiny, bird-like hands. She was petite and frail in stature, as well as strong and resilient in character underneath the surface.

∽∾∽

The usual schedule for Thanksgiving Day in our household began with everyone going to the ten o'clock Mass at our local parish church. Getting everyone ready in time certainly was a chore—borderline a frenzy, especially given Grace's extensive bath, medicine, and dressing procedures and also because good old mom was simultaneously preparing the start of the Thanksgiving meal. Thank goodness, Gamma helped so much with everything. The Thanksgiving Mass struck the perfect chord for the entire day and, upon reflection afterwards, made so much sense, especially when we take note that the word "Eucharist" means thanksgiving. Even though turkey day wasn't a required day of religious devotion, going to Mass on Thanksgiving Day seemed like a natural fit. Also, it was nice to celebrate the holiday with a few fellow parishioners, all part of the extended parish family. On top of all that, our little Grace loved going to church.

The key for us in preparing each year for Thanksgiving dinner was cooking all the dishes during the days before, including, of course, the big turkey. Over the years, my wife had become a master of preparing the Thanksgiving meal in advance, so that we could simply warm things up on Thanksgiving Day. This way also, my wife could attend to all Grace's needs throughout the holiday. Of course, everyone else in the family chipped in as best they could with tasks like setting the table, cutting the turkey, warming things up, filling the water glasses, and doing the dishes afterwards.

∽∾∽

My wife and I sat in the hospital room in the uncomfortable vinyl chairs over by the window and listened to the construction noises involved with the building of the new parking garage for the hospital. Together, we waited patiently for the doctor in charge to make his Sunday morning rounds. We were anxious, tired, and concerned. Grace, meanwhile, was fast asleep in her hospital bed, resting comfortably. As we waited, we filled the time by discussing, with optimistic hopes, the plans for Thanksgiving Day, the intended menu, and who exactly we expected to attend. All plans, of course, hinged on Grace's health and recovery, but we needed to plan just in case. We'd learned to expect the worst in life, but plan for the best case scenario anyway.

My wife reviewed, out loud, the list of people expected, "Let's see… you and I, Shannon and Grace, God willing, my mother, Great Aunt Gertrude, my brother Jimmy, and two of your sisters. That makes nine altogether for Thanksgiving." She stopped talking, but seemed to go on calculating and making all kinds of additional mental notes. My wife usually prepared for the Thanksgiving holiday for weeks in advance. The dining room table was usually set for Thanksgiving the day after Halloween.

The doctor in charge finally came into the room around 12:30 in the afternoon, still in the middle of his morning rounds. He seemed rushed. He quickly read the clipboard attached to the end of Grace's bed, acting as if no one else was in the room. He appeared reluctant to talk at first; then, he went about examining Grace, who lay there quietly.

Eventually, he turned toward us. "I think the new antibiotic is finally working, folks," the doctor said and then paused for reactions. The simple, concise statement cut the tension in one fell swoop. We both sat back with a sense of relief. The doctor then continued, "Her temperature is considerably lower and her white blood cell count has been drastically reduced. I think she's out of the woods now. I think, most likely, she'll be back to normal and home again in about two to three days. Fingers crossed and assuming no setbacks, she should be able to be home for Thanksgiving."

∽⌒∾

As everyone sat down for our Thanksgiving dinner—still called dinner, even though it was three o'clock in the afternoon—Grace's younger sister Shannon had decided that before anyone ate anything, she wanted to tell us what she had learned in school that week about the important November national holiday. Shannon was a nine-year-old, energetic fourth grader, who never had a shy day in her life.

Shannon stood up at the dining room table and read from her prepared note cards: "The Pilgrims came to America from England in 1620 and settled in the town of Plymouth, Massachusetts, which is named after the place they came from in England. The Pilgrims suffered a great deal in the New World, but during the following fall season, they celebrated a legendary harvest feast with the local Indians. Together, they had long wooden tables, white table clothes, a big turkey, and all kinds of vegetable crops from the soil, stuff that they had grown themselves such as corn, carrots and squash." Shannon looked around the table and then back down at her notes to continue. "The outdoor feast was an idyllic, harmonious celebration of nature's bounty and God's grace." Shannon finished her little presentation, quite proud of herself, and looked over at her older sister seated along the wall in her specially adapted highchair. Shannon added as she sat down, "There's the word 'grace' again, Mommy. It's everywhere." There was a silence at the table as everyone digested the little history lesson.

"Can we eat yet?" asked Great Aunt Gertrude, her bold inquiry breaking the silence. She sat with her knife and fork upright in the prepared position, as if ready to attack. She was famous in family circles for being a bit demanding, especially in restaurants around the country—places visited on holidays and family vacations together; the short list including the Plaza in New York City, where she once was asked to leave the dining room for complaining too much about a bent utensil.

"Not quite yet, Aunt Gertrude," I said. "Let's first say grace before the meal." I looked over at Shannon to acknowledge the use of that key, integral word yet again. "And, I'll do the honors." I took a sip from my water glass, folded my hands on the table, and then proceeded. "As Shannon reminded us all earlier, Thanksgiving became an official national holiday back in 1863 when President Abraham Lincoln declared the day to be a national holiday in his famous Thanksgiving Proclamation. And as we all know, Thanksgiving is a day to give thanks and to reflect on all our blessings. So Dear Lord, we pray that you help us to appreciate what we have, to always do our best in life, to inspire us to help others whenever we can, to enjoy this beautiful fall day, and most of all to enjoy this wonderful meal." After a short pause, I looked over at my wife and added, "Oh, and God bless the cook! Amen!" With that our family dug in.

The meal included lots of turkey, mashed potatoes, gravy, a special cranberry concoction with tiny orange slices, homemade coleslaw, string beans, dinner rolls, and best of all…homemade stuffing with warm apple chunks that Gamma had made.

After dinner was finished, I turned toward Grace and asked, "Grace Margaret, dear, are you having a nice Thanksgiving?" She, meanwhile, had eaten her pureed version of the full meal, which her mother had fed her prior to everyone else sitting down. Grace sat there quietly now, playing with a long ribbon in her hands while listening to one of her favorite music tapes. Hearing her name, Grace turned toward me, paused, and then replied in her own particular nonchalant, yet joyful fashion. She said simply, "Picnic."

∽∾

Question for the reader:

1. What does the title mean?

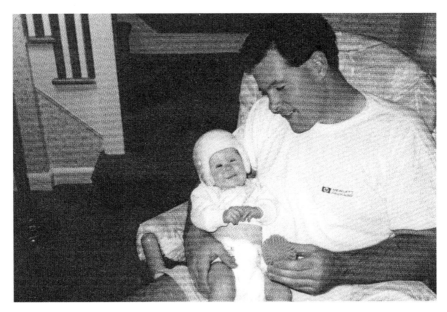

Grace as a baby, wearing her cranial molding helmet to protect her head and to help prevent her head from becoming misshapen.

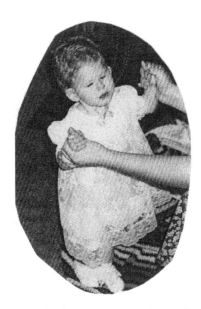

Grace at her Baptism, which was the same day as her sister Shannon's.

Grace as a small child, dressed as an angel and ready for Halloween.

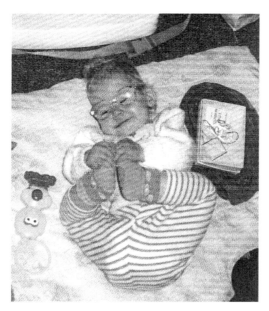

Grace as a toddler, wearing her special vision therapy eyeglasses (which never stayed on for very long).

Grace one Easter in her therapeutic stander to help strengthen her legs.

Grace with her mother only a short time after Grace's cranial vault expansion surgery.

A picture of the Millennium Jubilee Mass for the Disabled celebrated by Pope John Paul II on December 3, 2000 in the Basilica of St. Paul's Outside the Walls in Rome, Italy, and where Grace was seated in the first seat of the first pew (note the tiny white legs in the bottom right of the picture).

Grace being handed to Pope John Paul II at the Jubilee Audience on December 3, 2000.

Grace being hugged and kissed by Pope John Paul II at the Jubilee Audience on December 3, 2000.

Grace floating on air in the sunshine.

Grace and her sister Shannon after the May Queen Procession ceremony, the year Grace was the May Queen.

Grace sitting quietly in prayerful reflection.

Grace and her parents dressed up for Beth's wedding, where Grace was a bridesmaid.

Grace and her sister Shannon. The photograph was used for the family Christmas card that year.

Grace on the day of her First Holy Communion, sitting in her stroller with her grandmother at her side.

Grace and her parents at a Christmas function.

Grace and her family in the chapel. The picture was used by the Archdiocese of Philadelphia in the 2010 Annual Report for Catholic Social Services.

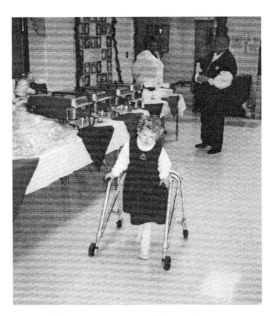

Grace using one of her walkers.

Grace on the day of her Confirmation.

A Christmas Concert

The evening performance was scheduled to begin any minute. I walked with my mother from the kitchen to the family room to take our assigned seats. My father, meanwhile, was busy getting organized and everyone else in the family scurried about with their designated tasks.

The family room of our house was especially cozy this year, appearing like a tiny Christmas village in a Charles Dickens classic, according to my father, anyway. The room displayed many Christmas symbols, themes, and blessings to celebrate the holiday in so many different ways. The room was always the heart of our house throughout the year and truly a special place during the holidays. It was my favorite room. First, the fireplace at the far end of the room crackled with a roaring fire, which not only warmed the room, but also soothed us with its array of colors, smells, and sounds. And, hanging on the mantel just above the fire, were three large red-and-white stockings, which belonged to my sissy and me and one for our little Yorkie Pebbles. We had emptied the stockings in a gleeful frenzy earlier that morning and opened all our presents from under the tree, as our parents sat on the couch nearby, yawning and drinking coffee. On the brick wall high above the fireplace, hung a beautiful homemade Christmas wreath with fresh fir and branches from real holly bushes. My mother had made the wreath from materials she'd purchased at a local farm stand. The wreath was about the size of a hula hoop (which, incidentally, is one of the Christmas presents I received this year) and it smelled like Christmas. On the extreme ends of the mantel there were large red Christmas candles placed in silver, angel-themed candleholders. The aroma from the burning candles could be smelled throughout the house. To the right of the fireplace, on the bookcase countertop about waist-high, my mother had a large wicker basket full of the Christmas cards we'd received in the mail this year; a few even included those sometimes dreaded long Christmas letters, which my father enjoyed reading out loud to us for fun on Christmas Eve, after a few spiked eggnogs. Beside the big card basket, my parents kept the radio and CD player, which filled the room with classic Christmas songs courtesy of the radio station that played them nonstop since before Thanksgiving. The song *Let it Snow* was now playing and we periodically glanced out the large family room windows into the backyard to see if our collective wish would come true. On the bookcase countertop to the left of the fireplace was our TV, which my father had on, but he had muted the volume while the holiday movie *A Christmas Story* played over and over on the one station all day long. We didn't need the volume, my father said, because he had all the lines of the movie memorized. My father was a big fan of the movie's main character, "Ralphie."

My mother and I sat on the extra chairs placed next to the piano, which was located at the extreme other end of the family room, away from the fireplace and along the wall closest to the kitchen. My father sat on the piano bench and started flipping through the old piano music book pages, looking for the first holiday selection to play. Propped on top of the old Baldwin piano was a large wooden Nutcracker soldier who stood proudly, as if protecting all those in the room from harm. I loved the Nutcracker soldier. My father and I respectfully called him "The Colonel."

My mother reached over toward me and gently said, "Okay, sweetheart, it's time for some fluids. Please open your mouth and let me give you a drink." Then she gave me a few sips from a plastic water bottle. I needed to drink a lot of water because my kidneys didn't work too well.

Just past all the extra seats, I could see the family room bar countertop, which displayed Christmas treats and goodies my father had received as gifts from some of his clients, co-workers, and friends. There were boxes of truffles, Christmas cookies, and chocolate-covered pretzels. There were also a few bottles of wine and some other things to drink, which my father referred to as "the hooch." In the back of all the items on the bar, propped up against the mirror, was my father's favorite book. It was a book about angels. The book had the angel Grace on the cover. Everybody says I look exactly like the angel on the cover.

Our Christmas tree was located up on the ledge in the living room, just thru the open French doors. I really loved our Christmas tree this year. My mother, Sissy, and I spent hours decorating the tree, one stage at a time, during the week before Christmas. I had helped with hanging some of the ornaments. My mother always decorated the Christmas tree in a simple, yet classy style, by first winding pretty small white lights around the tree, and then hanging beautiful big red bows, and finally placing select angel-themed ornaments. On the top of the tree, was a large golden angel with curly blond hair and a flowing white dress. She was beautiful. My mother loved angels.

With my being a handicapped child, it makes many things a little different for my family around the holidays. I'd have to say it's hard for everyone; but I figure we do our best. Everyone has to chip in a lot and help out because my everyday care is pretty involved. They don't seem to mind, though. See, I have a lot of health problems and I get sick a lot. I was born with a condition called hydrocephalus, which they tell me means water on the brain…whatever that means. I'm considered profoundly handicapped by the doctors, both physically and mentally. I have a shunt in my head. As I mentioned, my kidneys have trouble sometimes. I've had a lot of surgeries. I still wear diapers, but I'm trying hard to solve that. I can walk some, but I need guidance, which is especially important since I'm considered legally blind. I can see a little, but the tests say not much. I get seizures a lot, which I think is the hardest part for everyone. I take seventeen medicine doses a day. I hate taking medicine, but I've learned to cooperate, because I know it's good for me. I try to talk like everyone else, but most of my thoughts come out scattered and rambled. It's weird, I think about something to say and then, for some reason, different words come out. But, I love to talk.

My father spoke out at this point, "All right everyone, please, take your places. We're ready to start the evening performance." It was my father's idea to have the family Christmas concert this year. He had spent many hours in the months leading up to Christmas, teaching himself how to play the piano. According to my mother, he would rush home on his lunch break from work and spend about twenty minutes every weekday, practicing and trying to learn how to play. Sissy and I were always at school, so we never saw him practicing. He had found some old beginner books buried in the piano bench. Reportedly, the piano had been in my dad's family for generations, yet none of us played. My mother said he wanted to have the concert because he knew how much I loved music and he figured it would also be a great family thing for us all to do together for Christmas. She also told me his learning the piano had been a very slow process, which she had listened to from the kitchen. Several times along the way, she had gently suggested that he should get professional lessons.

See…there are a lot of things I can't do very well and a lot of things I don't like to do; but I love music. In fact, somehow, I have the ability to remember songs, the beats and lyrics, when no one else in my family can remember them. My father says a certain part of my brain works extra well because of my other problems. I don't know. I just know I love music. My father says I am like a beautiful songbird that has a wounded wing and can't fly like the others. I love music and I love going to church. I just can't explain why. We had all gone to Mass together on Christmas Eve. It was wonderful.

My parents tell people that I'm an angel from God. I think they are exaggerating, of course, but I certainly like hearing them say it. As a result, though, our entire house is filled with all kinds of angel things all year round. Even on the wall above the piano we have a large *Amazing Grace* song picture with an angel in it. My mom says I'm an angel, also because I look like an angel. She loves to tell people about my curly blond hair, porcelain white skin, and blue eyes. My favorite item in the family room, though, is the picture of me hanging on the wall. It's a picture of me and Pope John Paul II. I met the Pope a few years ago in Rome, Italy, back when I was a kid. I'm sixteen now.

My sissy is a freshman in high school and fourteen months younger than me. She is completely obsessed with electronics these days. For Christmas, she wanted a BlackBerry cell phone and a new laptop computer. I don't use that stuff, so I can't say much, but she sure was excited when she got the new laptop under the tree. She spent an hour Christmas morning doing a video webcam thing with one of her classmates. Myself, I'm happy receiving music tapes and CDs to listen to, ribbons and strings to wrap in my fingers, and warm snuggly pajamas.

∽

My father cooked Christmas dinner again this year for our family. He made baked striper (which is a fish) with butter and Old Bay seasoning. He served the fish with steamed broccoli on top. That was the first course. The second course was my dad's homemade spaghetti sauce with pork tenderloin and sweet Italian sausage mixed in. He served the spaghetti sauce over homemade cheese ravioli that he'd purchased from the Italian deli store in our town. He and Sissy waited in line for over an hour to get the ravioli and the fresh baked Italian bread. I can't eat regular foods unless they're pureed, but I loved listening to my father describe the menu. My food is prepared a lot like the baby food in the jars.

My father cooks for Christmas each year, so that my mother can focus on me and my needs. It gets pretty busy, especially with the diaper changes every two hours, all my medicines, and the constant water necessary. Keeping me hydrated is really important because my kidneys are scarred from prior infections. Everyone helps throughout the day with our Christmas. My Gamma runs the kitchen and helps my father with the cooking. My sissy helps set the table, takes care of Pebbles, and fills the water glasses. My Great Aunt Gertrude, Aunt Casey, and Uncle Jimmy all work together clearing the table, washing the dishes, and cleaning up the kitchen after the meal. Uncle Jimmy also watches the fire while my father is cooking. For dessert this year, we had a special apple cobbler that my Gamma had made. It was a recipe she'd learned from her grandmother.

During dinner, we played a game my father created of naming famous Christmas songs and carols. My Gamma brought a book with her to our house that listed them. She started the game with naming the song *White Christmas* because she said she loved Mr. Bing Crosby. My Great Aunt Gertrude had gone second in the game and quickly said, "*The Wizard of Oz*," so we had to explain the rules of the game again to her. Throughout our dinner, we went around the table several times and everyone listed some other really great songs including: *Rudolph the Red Nose Reindeer, Joy to the World, The Twelve Days of Christmas, Silent Night, The Most Wonderful Time of the Year, Chestnuts Roasting on an Open Fire, Frosty the Snowman, Jingle Bells, Santa Claus Is Coming to Town, Oh, Come All Ye Faithful, Deck the Halls, The little Drummer Boy, O' Little Town of Bethlehem, The First Noel, O' Christmas Tree, Blue Christmas, Jingle Bell Rock,* and the music from the "Charlie Brown Christmas Special," which is one of my particular favorites. I always feel bad when Charlie Brown tries to kick the football.

For my Christmas dinner, I had pureed turkey, green beans, and sweet potatoes, and then my Gamma's apple dessert mashed up. It was all quite delicious. My mother has to puree all my food because I have trouble swallowing lumpy textures. Basically, I can't swallow regular foods because of my disabilities. They say I'm "orally defensive."

We had already had one music concert earlier, before our three o'clock dinner, which my father called the "afternoon performance." He played three songs: *Jingle Bells, Silent Night,* and *Joy to the World*. I led the singing and we all sang as loud as we could. My Great Aunt Gertrude sang the loudest, and a few times she had trouble remembering the words. I helped her out, though. The earlier concert went pretty well overall. Afterward, my father jokingly compared us to the Vienna Boys Choir and the New York presentation of the Metropolitan Harmonic, whatever that all means.

On Christmas Eve, we had all watched a Christmas movie where the over-sized elf character in the movie kept saying, "The best way to spread Christmas cheer is to sing Christmas carols." I totally agree with that statement. On top of our TV, my mother had put a Santa statue. The chubby red Santa had a big bag of gifts over his shoulder. He had rosy red cheeks and was smiling. I love Santa. After watching the Christmas movie on Christmas Eve, my Gamma read to me in the family room until I became sleepy. She read to me Christmas stories from the storybook she had when she was a child. My Gamma always reads to me.

∽∾

My father made a big point when he said the prayer grace before our Christmas dinner, stressing how we all needed to keep "Christ" in Christmas. He talked about how so many people get caught up with all the gifts and presents and the commercial side of the holiday and, therefore, lose sight of the true meaning. My father reminded us to all try to act like Jesus. He quoted the homily from the priest from Christmas Eve Mass. Then my father told a few Santa jokes while we ate our first course. My father likes telling jokes.

The "evening concert," as it turned out, was the same three songs as earlier and we all enjoyed ourselves very much. Sissy rang little bells, keeping to the beat of the songs. Great Aunt Gertrude acted again like she was performing on Broadway and entertained us with her dramatic personality. Gamma stood next to me and held my hand. My Mother and I sat side-by-side in the chairs, leaned in toward each other, and sang to each other. My Aunt Casey sipped on a cup of eggnog between songs and took photographs. Uncle Jimmy waved his hands like he was the conductor. My father did pretty well with playing the piano this time. He only messed up a few times and we pretended like we didn't notice.

After the evening concert ended, my father turned to me for the little "finale" he wanted to do. We had been practicing together. He said to me as a cue, "Grace, sweetheart, what do you say now to everyone tonight for a special Christmas *blessing*?" He emphasized the word "blessing," I think to try and trigger my word association skills for the answer. I knew what he wanted me to say as a reply, but for some reason, I blurted out something totally different instead. I said, "Bunny rabbits, birds, pine cones, and cheeseburgers." I don't know why I said those things, but I just don't always say what I intend to say. It's a little frustrating.

But, my father was patient with me and like a lot of times, he just tried again, "No, Grace, let's try again. What's our special *blessing* for everyone?" He leaned toward me closer and he started the saying in order to help me get going. He whispered in my ear, "God bless us...." I suddenly remembered what he wanted me to say and this time I blurted out, "God Bless us every one!"

✌

Question for the reader:

1.   How does the word "concert" work on several levels in the story?

KNOWING GRACE

The day started out as a fairly typical Sunday, at least for me and my family. I got up around 6:30 A.M., showered, shaved, and dressed as quickly as I could. I'm an usher at the 7:30 Mass and supposed to arrive at least fifteen minutes early in order to greet the people as they entered. The technical name these days in the Roman Catholic Church is called a Minister of Hospitality; however, I still liked to be called an usher myself and my early morning team of religious rebels preferred our own methods of operation. For example, we refused to wear the name tags given to us and we never went to the organizational meetings. Anyway, as I rushed out the backdoor of our house that morning, I grabbed my windbreaker and a Sunday collection envelope from the drawer next to the refrigerator. I then headed for my weekly dose of redemption. As I walked briskly to my car in the driveway, I stuffed a twenty dollar bill in the envelope and licked the flap. Then, I jumped in the driver's side, closed my door, and sped off to church…safely.

The Mass went pretty much as I expected. It was quick, fulfilling, and enjoyable in a certain way. Candidly, though, I spent part of the time waking up from the prior evening. My wife and I had been up in the New Hope area, having drinks with friends, after taking a refreshing walk across the bridge and along the river. My wife and I hadn't been out together on a weekend for an evening with friends in well over a year, mostly the result of our generation being so busy with our young children and their activities. We had a nice time.

After the Mass ended, some of the 7:30 regulars congregated in the parking lot as was our custom and made small talk. We discussed the usual topics, which included the anticipated weather for the day, the latest happenings in the parish, recent Archdiocese news, and township politics, which usually got everyone riled up. After a few minutes of the typical idle chitchat, I begged off politely and walked to my car, even though I truly enjoyed the weekly discourse. However, I was a little pressed for time this particular Sunday morning. My plan was to get out to the Villanova area by 10:45 that morning, and I had one stop I wanted to make.

On the ride out, I intended to stop at the big chain bookstore located on Lancaster Avenue, which was just around the corner from our daughter's school. I had heard there was a new Irish anthology book available for sale, containing the best short stories from the Emerald Isle from the preceding year. I loved reading short stories, especially by Celtic writers. I also wanted to grab a café latte grande to help wake me up before I picked up our daughter at exactly 10:45, which was the normal pickup time for various reasons. For one thing, Grace's school had a 10:00 Mass in the chapel, which she usually attended, along with the nuns, nurses, administration, staff, and medical aides. They took all the non-contagious kids (those without the flu or a cold) to Mass each Sunday. The cozy little chapel was generally a parking lot of wheelchairs on Sunday mornings; the Mass itself full of noisy interactions coming from the special needs children, who prayed and sang in their own unique way. I generally tried to plan my pickup arrival each week for exactly when the Mass was letting out and, therefore, when everyone was exiting the chapel. That way, I got a chance to say a few hellos as I also swooped in to pick up our Grace. On occasion and especially on holidays, our whole family attended the Mass in the chapel together.

As I exited our parish parking lot in Richboro, Bucks County, I checked the inside of my car to make sure I had everything I needed for the trip, and fortunately, all seemed in order. In the cup-holder was my cell phone, which is a mainstay these days, of course, for everyone, but a particularly vital necessity for me on Sundays, in case of an emergency while driving with Grace. In addition, I had the black carry bag containing the portable oxygen tank. Inside the black bag is where we kept the instructions for operating the tank gauges and the CPR training materials from the classes my wife and I attended each year. I generally rehearsed the instructions each week on the drive out to the Villanova area, talking out loud to myself. If I didn't practice, I always seemed to forget the precise order for administering CPR, despite the fact that the instructions were given to you using the simple ABC acronym. And, taped to the front of the black bag was today's list my wife had written out to remind me what items to bring back home with me. I also had a large towel in the car, just in case Grace threw up during the car ride, which, unfortunately, she had a habit of doing for many different reasons and usually without any prior warning. Finally, in the back seat, was the customized, over-sized car seat we needed to transport Grace since she was now more than fifty pounds. Fortunate for me, *this time* I had remembered to transfer the car seat from my wife's car to mine the night before. I hated when I forgot to bring the darn car seat. Turning around when I was about halfway there and going back for it was really quite aggravating.

Normally, on my Sunday mornings drives, I listened to the radio. So, I pressed the far right button on my pre-set stereo dashboard looking for Philadelphia station 1210 AM, which to me meant "Sundays with Sinatra." I was constantly amazed how the old-time big band music made me feel so relaxed. It was the perfect recipe for a quiet Sunday morning drive on the relatively empty highways. I came to realize that I truly enjoyed the 1940s music, probably because it gave me the calming feel of the United States as depicted in the simpler times of the post-World War II era. And, I also knew that on the return trip home with Grace, I'd be listening to my daughter's favorite nursery rhyme songs on the tape I had all ready to go in the car cassette player. The child absolutely loved nursery rhymes. Those classic nursery rhymes often re-played over and over in my head during the work week. Not my favorite thing, perhaps, but they do grow on you and they certainly made our special needs daughter happy. Feeling somewhat prepared overall, I made my way through the EZ Pass toll and proceeded westbound onto the Pennsylvania Turnpike, also known as Route 276.

After a short while, I followed the signs and got on the "Blue Route," the alias for Route 476 south, headed for Villanova. The Blue Route was the southbound portion of 476, with the northbound portion being known as the "Northeast Extension," which headed upstate toward Allentown and the Pocono Mountains. Right about that time, the song *When I was Seventeen* started playing on the radio, which was one of my all-time Sinatra favorites. I drifted somewhat in nostalgia and I started singing along, doing my best "old blue eyes" impersonation. I had a thing about attempting impersonations of famous people which, in truth, usually weren't all that good. Meanwhile, I made a mental note to myself not to drive over the fifty-five mph speed limit because, from what I had observed on past Sunday mornings, speeding was not a prudent thing to do on the Blue Route. For some reason or another, the State Troopers always seemed to be on high alert for speeders at that particular time and place.

My mind eventually filled with the purpose of my trip—Grace, our oldest child. Our Grace was seven years old and, unfortunately, severely handicapped. Her numerous disabilities were both physical and mental and the list was long. While I hated using the "R" word with a passion, she was considered profoundly retarded and was also legally blind, all due to a primary condition from birth called hydrocephalus, which means water on the brain.

Born on All Saints' Day in 1994, Grace had been a medical quagmire ever since her traumatic birth. The actual delivery had been a horrific experience by itself. Our little Grace barely made it through alive. But, she defied the odds, which she has continued to do ever since. She has truly gone through a lot in her life. In the first two years of Grace's life, for example, she was hospitalized ten different times for all kinds of different problems.

Her daily care at home was completely overwhelming and incredibly complicated. My wife counted, in the daily journal she kept, more than 150 appointments in a single year for either a doctor's appointment or some kind of therapy. Grace basically needed twenty-four hour a day care. Many of the issues derived from the fact that Grace's bodily systems (bladder, kidneys, and bowels) simply did not work properly and she needed a medicine to help almost everything. The most basic things for Grace were difficult and an effort. The initial prognosis was that she would never develop past the infant stage.

During those early years, my wife worked tirelessly day and night to do everything necessary for Grace. I marveled at her love and dedication. She truly gave 110 percent and, in many ways, kept our daughter alive when the circumstances looked bleak. But even with my help and the help of many others, the carousel of medical care and medical problems never seemed to stop for a minute. A growing fear started with my wife, where she constantly worried about making a single mistake that could lead to a tragic result for Grace.

When Grace was three and we also had a younger child crawling around, I became increasingly concerned. The situation was simply too much. I started to worry about my wife having a nervous breakdown. She wasn't sleeping well. She wasn't eating much. She was constantly exhausted. All she did all day every day was take care of Grace, even when the medical aides and therapists were there to help. In addition, my wife was often up at night, calling various support groups and doing her own medical research, trying to determine the initial cause of Grace's problems. My wife constantly evoked theories to anyone who would listen, usually somehow blaming herself for something she might have done or didn't do during the pregnancy with

Grace. She was reaching for answers and beating herself up about something we later learned was all due to unfortunate genetics.

So, my wife and I started looking at other options outside our home and, after an extensive search for an appropriate facility, we made the difficult decision to place our Grace in a Catholic residential care facility for multi-handicapped, medically fragile children. The painful placement decision broke our hearts in pieces at the time and, perhaps, was not what every set of parents would have done given the same situation; but, it was the right decision for us. The special, nursing home-like facility, known as St. Michael's, was located in Rosemont, Pennsylvania, basically just down the road from Villanova University. St. Michael's was run by an order of nuns and the Archdiocese of Philadelphia, under the umbrella of Catholic Social Services. According to many with whom we spoke, the facility was one of the best of its kind in the entire country.

My wife and I considered St. Michael's like a nursing home for a loved family member, necessary because of the difficult circumstances. We also rationalized that the placement was sort of like sending our daughter away to the best college in the country for her…just much earlier than we had planned. We eventually referred to the facility as Grace's "school." Overall, St. Michael's became a godsend for us. They had around-the-clock nursing care, sophisticated equipment for the handicapped, and every kind of therapy one could imagine for special needs children—physical therapy, feeding therapy, vision therapy, sensory therapy, occupational therapy, etc. It was a setting where she could get all the therapy she needed, be around other children with similar problems, and have a nurse available at all times in case something happened. On top of the excellent care they provided for her and fortunately for us, our Grace absolutely grew to love it there. We were lucky.

Driving along on the highway this particular Sunday morning, I reflected on how it had been several days since I had last seen our little Grace, and I craved for her companionship. Our summer schedule at the time was that Grace came home each weekend for Sunday and Monday. Therefore, we spent those two days just concentrating on Grace's care and nothing else. When Grace was at home, I usually made the meals for the family and did the dishes. Meanwhile, my wife basically performed the job of four different people (she was the nurse, medical aide, therapist, and special dietary cook for Grace's food). My wife then would drive Grace back to St. Michael's on Monday evenings, while I took care of our younger daughter Shannon. Despite the immensely complicated and difficult care, spending time with Grace at our home on the weekends was the truest joy I had ever come to know, but, perhaps, a little hard to explain to others. Kind of like a puppy love or a tragic loss, you just know the feeling when you experience it. While I hated the fact that Grace wasn't with us every single day of the year, I focused on those two days a week when she was home.

෨෨

The biggest problem for us overall, was that our Grace was sick a lot. The poor kid has been sick or in the hospital about half of her life. By the age of seven, she had been hospitalized twenty-eight times in total and that included four long admissions for serious major surgeries. She received seventeen doses of medicine a day. She currently has fifteen doctors, including as follows: the primary physician/internist/pediatrician; neurologist; neurosurgeon; plastic surgeon; ophthalmologist; orthopedic doctor; ear nose and throat (ENT) doctor; urologist; nephrologist; audiologist; gastroenterologist (GI) doctor; dermatologist; dentist; infectious disease specialist; and child psychiatrist. And that does not even count all the genetic research doctors we consulted with after Grace was born. Each of the specialists in their own particular category of expertise had been a huge help in Grace's life and development. At various critical points, many of the doctors had already helped save her life.

Making it a point to drive carefully and within the speed limit, I traveled in the far right lane on 476 south and passed the exit for Route 76 (the alias for the Schuylkill Expressway), which was the way toward Center City. All the "76s" in the Philadelphia area roads must drive visitors to our city crazy. Anyway, at that particular juncture, I peeked at the grocery list of sorts provided by my wife, taped on the black bag and I read it out loud. Today's list had six items on it. In truth, I always asked for a list. It was important to be prepared...that was our family motto, which we had learned because of our Grace's problems.

The first item mentioned on the list was Lactulose, which was the daily medicine that helped with our daughter's bowel problems. Her bowels simply didn't work without the medicine moving things along. The second item was some pediatric enemas, for the same general bowel-assistance purpose. Third on the list was a reminder to pick up a dozen or so oversized diapers. Fourth was the Phenobarbital, which was the seizure prevention medicine. Fifth was her leg mafos, much like orthopedic braces and which helped Grace to walk. She had finally started walking some at age six and the mafos were inserted into her shoes to help with support. Last on the list was her walking helmet, similar to a generic bicycle helmet, but made for a special needs child. Grace needed to wear it whenever she walked, in case she fell. She was considered "legally blind," although she could see a little and she truly loved to walk, which was kind of a dangerous combination. Fortunately, Grace had become a pretty "sturdy walker" over time and a very "careful faller" as I often said to people when they asked. But, given her limited vision, we took no chances. I was curious whether or not my wife had meant to also put Pediasure on the list, so I reminded myself to ask the nurses for some of that, as well. Pediasure was Grace's liquid nourishment in a can. At each meal, she generally ate what amounted to a bowl of stage-one baby food and drank a bottle of Pediasure formula mixed with water. Because of her disabilities, she was "orally defensive." Therefore, Grace could not eat regular foods. It was hard for her to swallow the lumpy textures, so everything for her had to be pureed. There were feeding therapists and nutritionists working with Grace and they really helped her make progress.

Feeding Grace her meals, giving her the baby bottles of Pediasure, getting her to drink her necessary daily allotment of water each day—necessary for her significant kidney problems—administering all the different medicines throughout the day, the constant diaper changes every two hours, and all the time keeping a diary of all the above activities ... made for a pretty hectic daily routine. And, that's when Grace wasn't sick. I just hoped and prayed she was feeling healthy this particular Sunday.

∽∾

Still driving, my thoughts wandered to other topics as I passed the Conshohocken exit. I started recollecting the series of events that had occurred only a few weeks prior, on the first Sunday in May. It had happened before through the years and I'm sure it'll happen again, but like a nasty storm that passes through the area, you batten down the hatches and do your best until its over. That particular May Sunday of recent memory, our Grace ended up being admitted to the big children's hospital downtown for a period of thirteen days. The well-known downtown hospital was a great place for sick kids I always said, but a place parents don't necessarily want to be…because, if you're there, you usually have a pretty big problem on your hands.

All the trouble started when I had been watching a Phillies-Mets spring baseball game on TV with Grace in the family room of our home. She was sitting in my lap, enjoying my rather mediocre imitations of baseball announcer Harry Kalas. I kept saying, "That baby's outta here!" and Grace would laugh.

That's when I noticed she felt very warm. I checked her forehead and the back of her neck. Before I could even call my wife in from the other room, our little Grace started throwing up violently—"projectile vomiting" as the medical folks define it. It's a good thing we always keep a towel handy in every room of our house for these, all-too-common, occurrences. My wife was busy at the time in the kitchen, measuring and labeling all of Grace's medicine doses and dispersing them into serving syringes for later use. My wife jumped like a nervous cat and ran frantically into the family room to help me. Like a sudden weather change, Grace's usual happy, talkative disposition quickly turned into a non-responsive situation. Grace became limp and things got scary. She started having convulsions.

Fortunately, though, we knew the drill to a certain degree. We had learned a long time ago to stay calm whenever Grace got sick. As soon as the seizure started, we called our neighborhood paramedics and calling 911 in our township was a pretty safe bet overall, as they normally had a great response time. We were thankful for that. Usually, the paramedics were on the scene in less than ten minutes. After calling for help, my wife and I placed Grace on her side and made sure her breathing airway was clear. My wife then undid Grace's diaper and gave her an emergency medicine suppository called Diastat to try and stop the seizure. After that task was accomplished, we moved Grace onto her back and worked diligently to get the portable oxygen apparatus working. In about a minute or two, we had the oxygen flowing with air and the mask on Grace's face to help with her breathing. The oxygen was operating well when the paramedics arrived. That turned out to be a crucial thing, too, because Grace had started to turn a slight shade of blue just before the bag first inflated. In the past, Grace had stopped breathing entirely a couple of times when she had a seizure, so the oxygen was critical. We carried it everywhere we went with Grace. Meanwhile, during all of this, our six-year-old daughter Shannon manned the front door of the house for us and greeted the paramedics when they arrived. Like an old pro, little Shannon led the strangers inside the house to help her big sister. "This way, fellas," she said. "My sissy is in here."

The worst part of these all-too-common seizure episodes was the fear that Grace would stop breathing or that the seizure wouldn't stop. Watching your child have a violent seizure is quite a difficult thing for a parent to see, no matter what the circumstances. Fortunately, this time, the Diastat did the job, once again and after about five excruciatingly long minutes, the upsetting seizure finally ended. Then the paramedics did their thing from there. They placed Grace on a transport gurney and we were on our way out the front door. Grace was loaded into the back of the ambulance. My wife accompanied them in the front passenger seat of the ambulance and I was instructed to follow behind in our car. I followed the siren and flashing red lights as we drove to the closest hospital to our house. That was the usual routine for several reasons.

Driving in our station wagon behind the ambulance that day, I immediately turned my attention to the expected next stage of the process—the emergency room procedure at the "local/outside" hospital. I checked to make sure I had with me the medical summary document about Grace we carried with us at all times. We created the six page medical summary, which told the doctors everything they needed to know in an emergency situation. The comprehensive document set forth Grace's complicated medical diagnosis, identified all her current medications, provided a list of all of her doctors and gave a brief history of all the hospitalizations to date. My wife updated the summary repeatedly throughout the year.

My wife and I both knew, all too well, that after about four or five hours of questions and examinations at the local hospital, after a review of years of medical care with doctors, a bevy of diagnostic testing, and various attempts to insert IVs into her tiny, already-blown, hard-to-find veins, that the well-meaning doctors there would inevitably shake their heads because of the complexity of the situation and politely suggest that Grace needed to go downtown to the big children's hospital. They would explain that course of action was best because she was so complicated and also because the doctors downtown knew her case better. We would then have to go through the transfer process. It was not a surprise really and no one's fault; just hard on Grace and on us. Most of the time, they were right, anyway—Grace did need to go downtown. Either way, though, minor health situation or major event, we always went.

When we finally arrived at the big downtown hospital for children and were assigned to an ER exam room, but before they started to ask about Grace's diagnosis and history, I quickly gave a copy of the updated medical summary to the doctor in charge who looked at it briefly and then remarked, "Wow, this is really helpful." He started to read her medical diagnosis out loud.

"Let's see," he said, and then continued, "severe mental retardation, maximal hydrocephalus, holoprosencephaly, a neurogenic bladder, neurogenic bowels, caudal regression syndrome, visual impairment, Arnold Chiari I syndrome, febrile seizures, microcephalus, hyperactivity, and impulsivity." He paused and then added, "Also, I see she has a VP shunt as well as a vesicostomy." I could tell his head was spinning, taking in all that data and background.

This time, though, it was clear to me and my wife right away that something major was in fact wrong with our Grace. This was no minor ear infection, no simple cold with congestion, not a bothersome bowel backup, no ordinary flu, and no regular simple virus. The initial symptoms were often similar, but Grace's behavior was the real telltale sign. This time, she was acting limp and lethargic and that was a very bad sign. The indications led me to surmise that the problem was most likely either another shunt malfunction or another severe urinary tract infection (UTI).

A shunt had been surgically placed in Grace's head when she was a week-old baby. This was done to save her life because of the cranial pressure and, therefore, enable the excess cerebral spinal fluid on the brain at birth, caused by the hydrocephalus, to empty down into her abdominal cavity. Thereafter, the shunt could get clogged or infected at any time. There was nothing we could do to prevent it. If not the shunt, the problem was likely with her urine. Grace had already sustained numerous urinary tract infections during her lifetime because her bladder did not empty out properly. The ugliest thing about all the "UTI's," was that Grace generally didn't display any symptoms these days until the infection got really bad and also reached her kidneys. A vesicostomy procedure had been done to Grace when she was two years old, which helped by creating a second constant outlet for her urine. It meant her bladder now emptied all the time through an incision made below her belly button. She had what they called a neurogenic bladder, which meant it didn't empty by itself; so, puddles of urine used to sit in the bladder without any help. The vesicostomy helped the urine empty the bladder all the time. However, the paradox of the vesicostomy was that while it "prevented" many urinary tract infections from occurring by keeping the bladder empty all the time; when Grace got a UTI totally by chance, the infection was full blown by the time we found out. Normal little girls would cry when they tinkled through the urethra because it burned. With the vesicostomy, the situation was different and because Grace was mentally disabled and born with a high threshold of pain, she did not complain. These days, our Grace never exhibited UTI symptoms until she was very, very sick, and the onset always happened so fast. Before the vesicostomy operation was done, when Grace was a little baby, she constantly had the UTIs and we would always know because she would cry terribly in a high-pitched suffering voice as she sustained the burning sensations. The ER doctor eventually advised us that Grace's temperature was up to 105.2 degrees and he looked worried.

⤮

Switching lanes, I shook off the unhappy remnants of that most recent medical nightmare at the same time I pulled my car into the bookstore parking lot. I then got out of my car and walked in. I headed right for the fiction section, which was located on the second floor, not far from the coffee shop. I loved reading short story collections, especially anthologies. As I made my way up the second floor steps, I was drawn to a book on a display table about Astronomy. For some odd reason, I stopped and picked it up. I was struck by the large picture on the front cover. The oversized cover displayed a burning comet traveling in a dark sky full of sparkling stars. A particular notion or question hit me as I stood there and stared at it. I had a tendency to get little philosophical at times. I thought, what is the wisdom in realizing that a shooting star won't last forever? Is one better off to simply appreciate the majestic beauty, which only lasts a short time, or is the smarter person actually sad, knowing that such incredible moments are fleeting? Perhaps ignorance is a helpful tool sometimes in life, be it better not to foresee the end result at all and merely observe the visual array in front of you; said another way in simpler terms, I thought *enjoy things while you can*. I eventually made my way to the fiction section, perused for a while and selected a book to buy. With my intended purchase in hand, I decided to head over to get myself a cup of coffee.

"What can I get for you?" asked the young girl probably in her early twenties, speaking politely from behind the coffee counter. She was swirling steamed milk in an aluminum pitcher as she looked back at me for my order. She appeared a studious type person; probably, I surmised, a student at one of the many excellent Main Line colleges. She added, "And do you have one of our bookstore membership cards?"

I replied, "I will have a café latte, in fact, make it a Grande please. And no, I don't have a membership card, just the coffee please." To be honest, I often got a little annoyed at everyone always asking me for membership cards and store credit cards.

"Okay, then, that'll be two dollars and fifty cents," the young girl answered, as she stared at me with a curious look. "Excuse me, sir, but are you Grace's dad?" I took a moment to see if I recognized the young girl before answering.

"I certainly am," I eventually responded with a clear sense of pride, as I also reached for my money clip in my pocket. "Why do you ask? How do you know our little Gracie?" While I was a little surprised at the inquiry here at the bookstore, I had gotten somewhat accustomed to being known in many circles as Grace's dad. I rather liked it when the situation came about, as any proud parent would. And our Grace, as it turns out, knew a lot of people, or perhaps I should say…a lot of people knew her.

The young lady explained, "Sir, I worked last summer as a camp counselor at St. Michael's, at Camp Sunrise," she said. "I absolutely fell in love with your daughter the moment I met her. She is precious. How is she doing?"

I thought for a moment and then answered, "Pretty good. She's had some tough spells recently, but overall she is doing fine. She plays, as you know, in a different league than most other kids. But, considering everything…she's doing quite well in her division. Thank you though for asking."

"Sir, I have to tell you something," the young girl went on. She grew serious and looked around to maintain a certain sense of privacy and decorum. "Your Grace is the most incredible little girl or person, for that matter, I've ever met. And the Rome story is unbelievable. I saw all the pictures from the Rome trip in her room at St. Michael's, and I got chills when I checked out the website (www.svdp-richboro.org/grace.htm). I showed the website to all my friends and family. And, I absolutely love the fact that you can see Grace's little legs with her white stockings in the first seat of the first pew for the Millennium Jubilee Mass for the Disabled at the Basilica."

"Yes," I replied, holding back a little wave of emotion. "Our trip to Rome was a magical moment for our entire family and it was Grace's big day. Something, we will never forget.…"

She interjected, "I'm sorry to interrupt you, but I have to tell you something else, sir. Your daughter…your Grace…she changed my life." The senior college student, then went on to tell me, in detail, how she had switched her major after the Camp Sunrise summer program experience. She had changed her intended college degree from business to special education. She had determined that she wanted to work with handicapped children for her career. She confided in me, with some visible emotion, that it was meeting Grace that had been the inspiration. Then she thanked me.

⌘

Once I arrived in St. Michael's driveway in Rosemont, Pennsylvania, at 10:45 A.M. sharp, exactly on time, I made the right turn into the pickup and drop off circle, thus, heading toward the main entrance. I pulled over to the extreme right as I always did, just short of the electric front doors, for easy access to load Grace and her overnight belongings into my car. As I got out of the car and headed toward the entrance, I noticed for perhaps the umpteenth time the little wooden sign in the flower bed off to the side of the front doors. The sign read LOVE GROWS HERE. It was such an appropriate sign.

"Hello there, Maureen, how are all the kids?" I asked, as I entered the inside lobby. I then signed the visitors' entrance log and then went to get a drink from the nearby water cooler. Maureen was working the front desk. She was the proud mother of seven extremely Irish-looking children. Her kids all had freckles and red hair. Maureen worked the front desk at St. Michael's a few days a week and was literally a fixture around the place. Her job was to answer the phones and greet the parents when they came to visit or pick up their children. Many of the parents visited rather than taking their kid's home for many different unfortunate reasons. The overwhelming degree of care involved often dictated that less-desired course. Maureen's unwavering smile gave all the parents a shot in the arm right away. On top of that, her mob of freckled-faced little leprechauns often volunteered some of their own free time and helped with the care of the St. Michael's children, as if they were extensions of their own family. *Pretty impressive stuff* I always thought.

"The aide went to change Grace right after church," Maureen said to me and then added. "Grace should be out in a minute. I think Charise has her today."

"Or, as Grace likes to say, 'Reesy'," I offered back with a little playful smile and referring to the aide involved. Grace couldn't pronounce some names exactly, so she often came up with her own version of nicknames.

As I stood there in the lobby of St. Michael's, waiting for my daughter to be handed over to me for her weekly trip home, I couldn't stop thinking about the glorious wonders of this "home" for severe, multi-handicapped children. More people needed to know about this place—what they were all about and the loving way that they took care of these extremely complicated disabled kids. These medically fragile children were the type of children that, generations ago, never made it through the birthing process alive. In previous eras, they died at birth. And, with all the tragic negatives going on these days within the Catholic Church, I thought people needed to know of the good things that the church did, such as places like St. Michael's. I always said that one trip to St. Michael's could change a person's life forever. They see what a real problem is, that's for sure. The cards these children are dealt for life is unfair and unbelievable. They give us the perspective. At the very least, I think people hug their own children a little tighter after visiting. When people thought about Catholic Charities, it was a place like St. Michael's that should come to their mind. In that vein, we were proud the way our Grace had become a little poster-girl of sorts for the Catholic Charities Appeal and for Catholic Social Services throughout the entire Archdiocese of Philadelphia. They were always taking her picture for some brochure, special mailing, or annual report. In our minds, she had become a little ambassador for the needs of the disabled.

I looked toward the doors for the girls' hallway and saw my Grace now walking toward me, in her usual awkward, yet determined fashion. She was wearing a dainty, yellow sundress with the straps barely staying up on her slight, skinny shoulders. She had on her walking helmet, complete with the butterfly stickers, which made me smile. Her thick, curly blonde hair was flopping out on all the sides of the helmet. I could hear her saying, "Dadde" repeatedly at the urging of Reese, the pretty Jamaican lady who was the aide with her and just one of Grace's many, many buddies. Some people concluded that Grace had almost a cult-like following.

As I observed the big smile on Grace's face, I couldn't help but feel a touched appreciation and a pride that I maintained my importance in her life despite the separation. I lived each day with a bittersweet dilemma. I vacillated between feeling the overwhelming good fortune that a place like St. Michael's existed for our Grace and was part of our world, so that we could live a somewhat normal life the rest of the week; and the harsh stabbing brutal pain in the realization that my beautiful, blonde-haired, blue-eyed, seven-year-old special needs daughter did not live with us all the time. She lived someplace else for at least five days out of every week and I hated that, even though I knew it was best for her and for us. Sometimes there is pain mixed along with joy.

I reached down and gave Grace a big kiss on the cheek and then I picked her up into my arms. We hugged for a few moments as a small crowd gathered around us. I spoke a few minutes with some of the staff, including Mary Jo, one of the many wonderful nurses at St. Michael's. She gave me the morning update about Grace. The nurses at St. Michael's often acted like surrogate mothers to our special daughter, as they did with all the St. Michael's kids. The nurses were amazing and so loving to the children. Then, with all my items checked off my list, I loaded Grace and her supplies into my car and we started on the return trip home. We left St. Michael's and made our way, retracing the proverbial popcorn path with the exception of the bookstore visit. The new book of Irish short stories I'd purchased was in the back seat of my car.

Driving back home, I sang with Grace in unison, the classic nursery rhyme lullabies on the tape. It was one of our favorite things to do together. We had fun doing the simplest things.

Occasionally as I drove, I would carefully turn my head around quickly to check on Grace in the back seat, which was necessary to do. She was fine. Grace looked so happy sitting in the back of the car, snug in her car seat, and playing with a long ribbon in her hands, while listening to her music. For all her difficulties, the kid loved music and she had great rhythm. She knew the words of many songs. I don't know how she did, but she did.

∽∾∾

As I headed back to our home in Bucks County, I had another graphic flashback of Grace's two-week long hospitalization the month before. What a truly terrible time that had been.

After Grace had been transported from the "local/outside" hospital close to our house to the big hospital downtown, the "vicious cycle" reared its ugly head again and the saga of Grace's medical care became, once again, vividly clear. The emergency room doctors downtown initiated a new set of tests all over again. The additional tests included more x-rays, CAT scans, ultrasounds, blood tests, and painful catheterized urine samples. They also stuck a needle in Grace's head, close to where the shunt was located, in order to take a sample in order to determine whether the shunt was infected. Further, they endeavored to put another IV in her wrist because the first one had already failed, which was like watching someone being tortured. It was always about ruling things out. When they tried to insert the IV, our poor little Gracie kicked and screamed like you couldn't imagine—or worse—like you could. She had received so many IVs by that point in her life that both wrists had tremendous amounts of scar tissue. It usually took three nurses to pin her down, hold her still, and get a good IV *stick* that would hold. Even something as easy as taking her blood pressure was difficult because Grace fought the intrusions to her body like her life depended on it.

Ever since the cranial vault expansion surgery, which was done when Grace was five years old, the poor kid didn't want any unknown people with surgical gloves anywhere close to her for fear of the associated pain. The cranial vault expansion surgery was one of Grace's most brutal hospitalizations. That was the operation where they had to break Grace's skull into pieces and then rebuild it. They needed to build a bridge in her skull plates in order to give her abnormal brain room to grow. If they hadn't done the procedure, she would have died, because of the increasing cranial pressure on her spinal column. After the six hour surgery, she had 240 stitches in the top of her head. It made you cry to look at what they did to her, but they saved her life.

The big children's hospital downtown is a teaching hospital, which is a great thing on one hand, but it also meant that we had to always go through the medical ladder learning process. First, we always answered the questions of the often wet-behind-the-ears "intern," who then relayed his or her impressions to the "resident" in charge, who eventually gave his or her diagnosis and/or opinions to the attending doctor, who hours later, came in and talked to us. They all carried around the Medical Summary we gave to them, sometimes as if they were trying to figure things out without reading it.

As great a hospital for children as we have in downtown Philadelphia, the system could always be a little better. That was generally true, I think, with hospitals in today's complicated health care environment. For example, that first night downtown, I ended up sleeping...or should I say sitting upright with my eyes closed...in the ER exam room all night long while the *ER Team* decided what to do with us. My wife went home in the early morning with our six year-old daughter Shannon for a few hours of rest. All I can say constructively is the emergency room chairs should all be convertible into pullout beds and they need to have pillows and blankets available for the family. Fortunately, I had one of my short story books with me, as usual, to keep me company.

We were given some test results on the morning of the second day. However, they told us they could not treat Grace, yet, with an antibiotic because they didn't know the exact infection involved. But, they did know two things so far: her kidneys were not functioning properly—she had a very high Creatinine level—and she was severely dehydrated. So, we were shipped upstairs to an available hospital room (nothing is as easy as you would think) and Grace was started on IV fluids and Tylenol.

Over the course of the next thirteen days, I worked at my office during the day and then came downtown to the hospital each night to relieve my wife, who had the dayshift. She stayed with Grace all day long, every minute. We basically exchanged the proverbial baton at around 6:00 P.M. and my wife went home for some rest. I would sleep in the hospital each night. One of the important things to know about Grace is that she could not be left alone for a single moment because of her unique combination of disabilities and abilities. She was legally blind and severely handicapped mentally, but she could walk, so she was not a patient that should be left in a hospital bed without supervision. Thank God, my mother-in-law was always at our house taking care of our younger daughter Shannon, during all these extended hospitalizations. So, I slept in Grace's hospital room each night, on a cot next to her bed. I then got up early each morning to drive back home for a quick shower and to go to work. I was fortunate in an odd way though—I didn't need an alarm clock. With all the hospital machine buzzers, beeping noises, and the constant vital sign checking by the nurses, it was virtually impossible to sleep for any length of time in the hospital. And, the backup wake-up call mechanism was the construction work going on outside my daughter's hospital room window, which usually began at 6:00 sharp each weekday morning. When the new parking garage finally gets completed, I will certainly have mixed emotions. It'll be nice to have a place to park, though.

Over the course of several days, we spoke with pediatricians, urologists, nephrologists, infectious disease specialists, neurosurgeons, neurologists, nuclear medicine consults, nutritionists, and the lab people when they called Grace's room; but we never received any conclusive answers. It was like being strung along in a Paul Newman con-artist movie. We were always getting closer to the coveted answer, but it never arrived. We always needed to do one more test to rule something out.

Eventually, with all the tests allegedly completed, we were finally waiting for the head of the Nephrology Department to get out of surgery and come tell us what the latest lab results indicated. At least, that's what everybody kept telling us we were waiting for. All of a sudden, a doctor walked in the room.

"Good afternoon, folks. I am the chief nephrologist here. My name is Dr. Hartnee. Has anyone from my team been in to see you today? What do you know so far?"

"No, doc," I answered for us, with a slight tone of sarcasm. It was a Sunday afternoon. I hadn't showered in two days. I was tired and cranky. "No one has been in to talk to us from nephrology today and we don't know Jack Sh…we don't know too much, doc."

"Okay, then," he said. "Let me explain where we are." He sat down in a chair and continued. "The cultures are all back and your daughter has a *whopping infection*. We believe the infection is an E-coli bacteria. We thought for a while she might have a bug called pseudomonas, but now we don't think so. Anyway, the infection is in the bladder, your daughter's kidneys and also in the bloodstream …we call that being septic, which is not good. Also, her kidneys are failing. At this point, her Creatinine level is ten times what it normally should be, which indicates that neither of the kidneys is working very well. The left kidney, as you know, is badly scarred from prior onsets of pyelonephritis. That left kidney might need to be removed entirely someday because we are noticing indications of high blood pressure, but we will talk about that possible procedure down the road. We've been trying to get her hydrated by giving her IV fluids. Now that we know the exact bug we are dealing with, we can start her on strong antibiotics and get going with treatment. Hopefully, we'll select the right antibiotic, because I know your daughter is immune to some of them from all her past encounters. I reviewed the long list of antibiotics she's had in the past which include: Suprax, Amoxicillin, Augmentin, Bactrim, Ciproflaxin, Ceftriaxone, Vancomycin, Zithromax, Clindamycin, and Erythromycin. And, up to now, we had to be careful to prescribe one, because as you know, a lot of antibiotics are damaging to the kidneys. Overall, she is a very sick little girl. But nothing we haven't seen before." My wife and I digested the information and I scribbled notes furiously on my little yellow legal pad.

"Doctor, let me jump in," I eventually said, as I caught up. "I follow you with most of what you just said. As you see, I've been sitting here taking notes for days now; but, when you guys say the kidneys are failing…don't you really mean kidney reduction? Don't you mean to say that the kidneys are not working up to capacity; because, the kidneys are still working somewhat, right?"

"Yes, Dad, very good point. The kidneys are still working to a certain degree. However, we consider the situation an acute renal failure. Your daughter's kidneys, even on a good day, do not work at one hundred percent capacity like a normal person, because of her birth abnormalities and defects, and because of the past scarring from infections; but they do normally work well enough to get by. As you probably know, some people can function with only one kidney."

"Which leads me to my next question, doctor," I said. "I compare the kidneys to being like a CD disc so that I can understand things. Every time our Grace gets pyelonephritis, she gets more permanent scarring, which uses up some of the available storage on the disk/kidney. Eventually, she's going to run out of storage, isn't she? How close are we to that unfortunate situation happening, doctor? God forbid."

"Again, good question. Let me answer that this way. We expect that we can get Grace back to the functional kidney levels that she had before this illness. How much permanent scarring results…we will have to wait and see."

Perhaps, tougher than any other aspect of Grace's stays in the hospital was the combination of how complicated she can be to treat, along with the present realities in the modern-day health care world. For example, every time the nurses changed shifts, we felt like we had to prep the new nurses ourselves and make sure they read her complete chart because Grace was often the exception to all the rules. As great as most of the nurses were, the fact is, a lot of nurses these days are only part-timers or they work in all the different hospital departments.

They are seldom specialized as much anymore. It's bad enough that the team of doctors rotates every so many days, which I understand is only practical, but some nurses, for example, only worked two days a month. How can any company run efficiently with key employees that only come in two days a month? And, of course, there are usually way too many patients for one single nurse during any single shift. In the thirteen days of that particular hospitalization we noticed several disturbing occurrences including: 1) the wrong antibiotics almost being administered, 2) the nurse forgetting to put the CR monitor on as ordered by the doctor, which was important in case of a seizure or a breathing disruption, and 3) some un-Godly delays in getting lab results back or medications delivered because someone along the chain got misinformed or simply dropped the ball. But, as I always say today more than ever, please understand that I am not complaining, I'm just commenting. These things did happen. But, overall, the care was excellent and the people involved truly cared about our daughter. Perhaps, the biggest point is that even the best hospitals can still improve. And another very fair statement is that the *parents* are a necessary and productive part of any medical team for their own children. My slogan is, "You gotta be involved."

∽∾

Pulling into the driveway of our home around noontime that Sunday morning, my thoughts turned to my optimistic intentions for the actual day in front of us. On warm-weathered Sundays, we usually planned for a picnic in our backyard. It was a simple recipe. I would set up lawn chairs, picnic blankets, and radio; and then we'd have lunch in the yard with our girls. After lunch was over, we would push the girls on the swings, lie around in the hammock over in the shade under the trees, play Wiffle ball or watch the two girls drive around the yard in Shannon's pink Barbie jeep. They both wore seatbelts and, hopefully, only Shannon did the driving. Of course, we now also enjoyed watching Grace walk around the yard and feel her own sense of exploration. All kinds of new wonders came along with her walking. The new addition to the backyard this year was the doll house/shed we had recently purchased. The concept was a doll house for the girls in the spring, summer, and fall and it would serve as a storage shed in the winter.

∽∾

Around four o'clock that afternoon, we had an unexpected visitor. We were in the backyard rolling around on picnic blankets, tickling each other, and giving each other raspberries, when our parish pastor, Father McDevitt stopped over to say, "Hi."

"Well, hello, Father," I replied, as I stood up and dusted grass off myself. "What a pleasant surprise."

"I was on my way to my mother's house for dinner tonight," he offered, "and I thought I'd stop in. I hope I'm not intruding. How is everybody doing today…and, especially, how is our Grace feeling?" He was a very kind and polite man. He really went out of his way and took a special interest in our daughter Grace.

I answered, "She is doing well and happy as ever, Father. We've been walking all over the yard, playing Wiffle ball and playing in the new doll house."

"Yes, I can see the doll house. It looks like a little Irish cottage; very nice."

"Father, would you like to sit down?" I then asked. "Here, take the Adirondack chair. I'll give Grace to you for a hug and to say hello."

"How are you Grace?" Father McDevitt asked as he sat down and called to her from a few feet way. She turned and walked directly toward him after hearing his voice. "How is our little TV star this afternoon?" he went on. Father McDevitt was referring to the fact that in December of each year, we usually took Grace to the annual Archdiocese Christmas Party that Catholic Social Services had for children. The Cardinal or Archbishop in office presided each year over the wonderful function, which included a Nativity play, music from a Catholic high school band, and a visit from the big guy himself…Santa Claus. All the Local TV news teams usually covered the event and some of the assigned reporters made it a point each year to put Grace on the six o'clock evening news. This past year when the news crew arrived, I heard one of the reporter's even ask in the back of the room, "Do you know where Grace Bowen is seated?" As a result, people often referred to our little Grace affectionately as a mini-celebrity.

"As you guys put it," Father McDevitt said, "there is nothing on this earth like a Gracie hug. What is it you say…a hug from Grace makes *you* feel better?" With that, Grace took a few steps toward Father McDevitt. As she got closer to him, her arms went out like wings and then she fell forward into his arms. She grabbed his neck with her skinny little arms collapsing tightly around the back of his head. She hugged him fiercely and at the same time said, "Father McEvit," which was her own version of our pastor's name.

Father McDevitt continued, "I told my mother that I would try to give her an update today about Grace," he said, as he was returning the hug back to Grace. "I didn't get a chance to speak with you after church this morning, so I figured I'd stop over. Mom has been praying for her, too, especially since that last hospitalization."

"Please tell her, Father, that Grace is pretty much back to her old self now and also please let your mother know we were all asking for her."

During the short visit that ensued, we spoke at length about Grace and Shannon and their upcoming summer events, which would include, for Shannon, the parish summer bible school classes. For Grace, there was the wonderful Camp Sunrise program at St. Michael's. We also spent a few minutes reliving some of our fondest recollections from our memorable trip together to Rome, Italy, back in December of 2000. Father McDevitt had joined us on the trip at the last minute, at his own expense.

"I will never forget that trip, as long as I live," said Father McDevitt. "I still show the videotape you gave me from the Papal Audience to parishioners, probably once a month at least. Thank you again, by the way, for the extra copy of the video. People now-a-days need to hear and see stories like that; it helps strengthen their faith."

"It certainly did that for us, Father. Now, I know how busy you are and how you probably have to get going soon. So, just let me know and I will walk you out front to your car. We really appreciate your stopping by, though. Also, I want to tell you an Irish priest joke on the way out."

"Okay, then," Father said, as he rose up. He then gave a short blessing for our family and started with me across the lawn toward the front of the house.

"Wait, let me get one more hug from Grace before I go," he said, as he walked back a few feet and knelt down. He softly whispered goodbye to our Grace, said a prayer and then warmly hugged her again. This time, though, she wouldn't let go of him.

"She's surprisingly strong, too, isn't she," Father remarked, as he let the hug take its well-meaning course.

"How about me, father?" spoke Shannon, as she ran over and positioned herself for a hug, as well. "You know you're the best hugger," she added. With that, our Shannon also gave him a big bear hug as he lifted her up off the ground in his arms. Truth was…Father McDevitt was the best hugger around. He loved to greet the little children of the parish with an affectionate and totally appropriate hug after Mass. He was a man of God and truly a man of the people. He loved kids for all the right reasons. He was initially a high school teacher by trade, a principal, in fact. In today's world especially, it was difficult on the loyal clergy to still be themselves. I gave Father a lot of credit for not changing his ways, just because of other people's faults and imperfections.

He turned toward me and said, "I still tell people your, 'Whose the best hugger story'. That's my personal favorite. I still use it sometimes in my homilies."

"It is not only a *great* story, Father," I quipped, "but as we know, a *true* story, as well. The Pope and the Cardinal will just have to share second place when it comes to giving out hugs. For my girls, you're number one and they've seen it all. Now, let me walk you to your car. I don't want your eighty-six-year old mother calling here looking for you." With that, we, as a family—my wife walking hand-in-hand with Grace—all escorted Father McDevitt out front to his car. Then, we all waved as he drove off.

∽∾

My wife and I spent the remainder of the afternoon sitting out back and working with Grace on her growing vocabulary. Her current repertoire included: bubbles, toys, birds, mommy, daddy, sissy, annon, go for a walk, outside, in the van, bam-bam, puppy, music, tapes, pope, wee, lap, yes, no, window, sun, raspberries, oops, telephone, stand up, hi, hello, love, steps, hugs, for a ride, baad-a-bing, and the most recently added scoobie-doobie-do. Sometimes, we couldn't figure out where she picked up some of the latest lines she came out with. She was remarkable, but in a totally different way than other kids. She couldn't do a simple math problem, but she could count to fifty if you alternated the numbers with her and she loved reciting the alphabet anytime, anyplace, with anyone. The other amazing thing with her we started noticing more and more was that she was now using words by association, which she had never really done before. Between us—her family—all the people at St. Michael's and her teachers at the Main Line School for the Blind, where she went during the week for special education, she received a lot of verbal stimulus. We often said, "We really shouldn't be surprised by her anymore."

At exactly five o'clock in the afternoon, my wife and I kicked into high gear for Grace's care. Special needs parenthood was calling our name. The first task was to change her diaper, which usually took two of us these days because Grace wouldn't stay still for a second; she was always grabbing everything, and the vesicostomy incision leaked urine all over the place if you weren't careful. So, one person kept her occupied by singing to her and blocking her flailing hands, while the other person did the actual diaper change. The next task was to give her all her 5:00 P.M. medicines. My wife was in charge of that department. I watched her give Grace syringes full of thick, colored fluids including: 1) Lactulose for her bowels; 2) Reglin to help with her digestion; 3) Phenobarbital for the seizure control; 4) Zantac to help her stomach because of all the other medicines she took; 5) Tennex to limit her hyperactivity; and 6) a big syringe full of her daily vitamins. In between the medicine doses, my wife gave her sips of water and dealt with her constant gagging, which often was just Grace's way of expressing displeasure with taking the medicine. In some cases, the behavioral gagging caused her to throw up, which left us pretty much back at the medicine starting line. We then had to try and figure out what medicine had been digested and what needed to be re-dosed. We had to be very careful too with administering the medicine. My wife kept track of everything Grace drank and ate everyday, as well as her bowel movements—all important information to keep an eye on because of the relevant medical issues.

After all the medicine was finally administered, my wife took over in the kitchen with the complicated, sometimes messy, yet very satisfying and essential job of feeding Grace her stage one pureed food. She only ate soft pureed foods prepared in advance and not much of that. Feeding her was definitely an exact science. You had to massage her mouth first to establish to her that a meal was coming. Then you asked her or coaxed her to open her mouth. If and when she did, we then informed her that it was time to *eat* while the food made its way in for an airplane landing. We had a special feeding chair for her with safety straps and a tray—like a big highchair. Sometimes, she would flail her arms and knock the food all over the place. We had all kinds of tricks and devices to keep her entertained while we fed her. For example, we always had a cassette player nearby playing her favorite songs. We also gave her ribbons for her hands to keep her busy. Finally, we put her in the sunlight over near the window because she loved feeling the warmth of the sun on her face. All in all, on most days, she ended up eating a little more than she threw. And, generally, she ate pretty well if she was feeling okay. Whenever she was sick, though, it was a completely different story. When she had a high fever or was vomiting for whatever reason, we couldn't get food, fluids, medicine, or anything else into her. That was why we were then looking into the prospect of having a feeding tube surgically implanted in her stomach. They call it a G-tube or a "button." If we did do this, we thought, maybe she would no longer have to be hospitalized just for fluids, medicine, and nutrition. However, ever since the cranial vault expansion surgery, just saying the word "hospital" and "surgery" made me cringe and I wasn't even the patient. We were still debating the G-tube idea.

When Grace was younger, we had dealt with all kinds of therapeutic devices, including a cranial molding helmet, eyeglasses to see if her poor eyesight would improve, an orthopedic stander to help her gain leg strength, therapy chairs for posture, and various different metal walkers—all designed for special needs children.

After a delightful supper, Grace was then given a warm, after-dinner bottle of Pediasure mixed with water. The bottle was served by Mommy and Sister Shannon working together as a team on the couch in the family room. All feeding efforts were conducted with the dual paramount goals of getting her to finish *and* somehow keeping her from regurgitating it back up. After the evening 'Bah-Bah,' we then placed Grace standing up in her playpen in the corner of the family room near the TV, for her to stand for awhile and digest her food. We then all tried to watch a little bit of a Sunday night Disney movie on television. As we sat in the living room for a few minutes of relative calm, I looked over to our "angel" display on the bar. That's where we kept most of our angel-related stuff. We believed in our souls that our Grace was an angel from God for a multitude of reasons. My favorite item on display was the *Believe* book about angels, which had pictures and poems for the different angels of distinction. The picture on the front cover of the book was the official Angel Grace, who had an uncanny resemblance to our daughter Grace—just one of the many angel-related coincidences.

Eventually, our little gang made our way upstairs (when Mommy said so) for the girls' Sunday evening bath together. Grace loved the water, so the bath was a fairly enjoyable experience for everyone. Daddy was needed at times to do the lifting in and out of the tub because Grace could become a fifty-pound dead weight with soap suds. When everyone was all dried off, we dressed them in their matching princess-themed pajamas and got them ready for bed. Mommy tried her best to brush Grace's teeth, which was another ordinary task that ran into a multitude of complications and issues because Grace was orally defensive. Again, we had to constantly weigh the competing factors of brushing the teeth as best as possible, but not so far as to induce a gagging episode and her throwing up. Teeth slowly and carefully brushed, Grace was then given her evening enema or suppository along with her post-bath diaper change. The enemas and suppositories were administered like clockwork three times a week, each on alternating nights. We preferred giving them to her in the evenings because changing constant dirty diapers every two hours at night was a tad easier for us when she was asleep or groggy. Either way, we had to get up and change her diaper throughout the night because of the enemas and also because her urine flow was constant due to the vesicostomy. If we didn't change her every two hours, we increased the risk for another UTI. Also, all the sheets in her special Vail safety bed with rails would be soaking wet by the next morning. Finally, of course, we couldn't have her sleeping in wet clothing.

∽∾∼

At around 11:30 that evening, my wife and I were finally getting into bed ourselves when I turned to her, smiled, and remarked what a nice day it had been. She nodded her head agreeing with me, although I could see she was utterly exhausted. She reached for and set her alarm clock a few hours ahead so that she could get up and change Grace in the middle of the night. She had the first shift. I had the second. My alarm was already set for 3:30 A.M. She and I sighed almost simultaneously as we both then talked about how tired we were.

After a few minutes, the discussion turned to the upcoming meeting my wife had with the county social worker assigned to Grace's case about Grace's IEP and IHP. The IEP (Individualized Education Program) and IHP (Individual Habilitation Plan) were extensive annual summaries that analyzed and implemented Grace's medical care needs and special education program given her age, disabilities, and health issues. The elaborate reports were generated from the annual meetings each fall and each report was well over forty pages long. Each year at the meetings, input was obtained from Grace's teachers, doctors, nursing personnel, and all her therapists. All the relevant aspects were addressed and then realistic goals for the ensuing year were designated.

At that point I said to my wife, "You know, I miss Grace so much when she's not here during the week and I often feel terrible that she does not live with us all the time; and, I truly love when Grace comes home on weekends," I paused and then went on. "But, I have to admit, she is *so darn complicated*. I wonder sometimes what other people would think."

My wife nodded, paused for a second, and then said simply in return, "I think they would just have to know Grace."

Angels on Earth

Angels are a gift to us,
They come from God above.
You'll feel them all about you,
When you live your life with love.

– John Wm. Sisson

Little Shannon picked the colorful, extra-wide book off the display shelf and carried it over toward her mother, who was standing at the back of the check-out line. Her mother had her hands already full of assorted items intended for purchase. This was her mother's favorite store—a quaint, angel-themed boutique located in the friendly and charming confines of Peddler's Village in Lahaska, Bucks County, Pennsylvania. Her mother collected angel-related keepsakes of all kinds and her intended acquisitions on this day included a few ornaments for next year's Christmas tree—some nice selections to add to her already impressive holiday collection. She also intended to buy several pink and white laced, angel-covered ribbons, and a packet of angel-themed writing stationery.

"Mommy, can we buy this book?" asked Shannon, when she reached her mother. Raising the book up to her mother, Shannon added, "The girl on the book cover looks just like Grace." Shannon was ten years old—a beautiful little girl, inquisitive and full of energy. She had long blond hair, chubby cheeks, and pretty blue eyes. Shannon was referring to her older sister Grace, age eleven, who had stayed at home with their father that particular Sunday afternoon.

"Oh my!" her mother responded. "That really *does* look like *our* Grace." Mrs. Bowen focused intently on the front of the book for several moments. The picture on the cover depicted a curly, blond-haired little girl set forth as an angel with porcelain skin, rosy red cheeks, thin ruby-colored lips, and blue eyes that sparkled. The beautiful seraphim had majestic large white wings flowing in the background behind her. After a few more seconds of contemplation, she answered her daughter.

"Yes, Shannon, sure; let's get the book." As Shannon handed the book to her mother, the two of them simultaneously moved up in the line and were now directly at the counter for the cash register. The middle-aged woman behind the counter had heard the exchange between mother and daughter.

The store employee offered, "Excuse me, ma'am, but I couldn't help but overhear your conversation, about the book you have there…. You know, the picture on the cover is actually a picture of the official Angel Grace. If you look down on the very bottom, in real small print below the picture, you can see the name inscribed."

Mrs. Bowen examined the cover more closely and then remarked, "Wow! That is so uncanny. The Angel Grace on this cover looks exactly like my daughter Grace, her older sister." She pointed at her youngest and then placed her intended purchase items on the counter.

"That's a little eerie and quite interesting, don't you think?" asked the sales clerk, as she starting ringing up the charges for the purchases. "We employees around here at this store, those of us who are rather religious and really into angels, we find significance in things like that little coincidence. Forgive me for asking, but does your daughter exhibit any special spiritual qualities?"

Mrs. Bowen smiled and looked over at Shannon, who smiled with a big grin, as well. Mrs. Bowen replied, "Our Grace…actually, I don't know where to start to answer that question because, you see, our Grace is a severely handicapped child and she is *extremely* spiritual. I could tell you stories all day long about how she inspires people and how she affects people's lives. She is a very religious person. For example, she absolutely loves going to church. We don't know why exactly, but she does. She loves to pray. And, well…she was born on All Saints' Day."

The store clerk took a short step backward and felt chills going down her spine. "Really!" the clerk asserted rather loudly and then asked, "What do you think the odds of all that might be? Her being born on All Saints' Day, her name being Grace, and her looking exactly like the Angel Grace. I would truly love to meet your daughter sometime, if you ever could bring her into the store. I know I've seen you in here from time to time."

Mrs. Bowen added, "Yes, well, maybe next time I come in I'll bring our Grace in to meet you. She has an amazing little personality, but she has a lot of medical problems. She's been through a great deal in her eleven years of life and she doesn't travel well for a lot of reasons. She's home today with her father. When we do take her out with us, we need to have at least two adults present in case she has a seizure somewhere or in the car while we're driving. She gets a lot of unexplained seizures. But that would be nice idea, though; maybe next time I'll bring her into the store."

The store clerk hesitated, but then added, "Forgive me for asking, but what are Grace's medical problems? I hope you don't mind my being so forward? I use to be a pediatric nurse at a big hospital downtown. I retired because of the terrible commute and the long shifts. I work here now part-time, mostly because a friend of mine owns this store."

"Well," answered Mrs. Bowen. She looked around to make sure there was no one behind her in line, plus she was thinking of where to begin. "Our Grace was born with a primary condition called hydrocephalus which, as you probably know, means 'water on the brain.' As a result, she is profoundly disabled both physically and mentally. She is also legally blind. But given everything, she is our little angel. And, she's also a little famous for a couple of reasons."

The store clerk looked utterly shocked. After an extended pause, the clerk excitedly said, "Wait a minute. You're not Grace Bowen's mother are you? Grace Bowen, the little girl who was hugged and blessed by Pope John Paul II in Rome, Italy, a few years back? I read about all that in the newspapers."

Mrs. Bowen became visibly emotional at this point. She nodded her head proudly, while also smiling from ear to ear. She started to speak, but the store clerk interrupted.

"I read all the stories and articles about your daughter in *The Philadelphia Catholic Standard and Times* and the *Bucks County Courier Times* newspapers. And didn't your family also go to *People Magazine* in New York? I have been following the articles about your Grace over the last few years. I remember them and I especially loved the line in one of the articles where someone said about your Grace, that 'when you hug Grace Bowen...*you* feel better'."

Mrs. Bowen and the store clerk went on talking for a while about Grace, her special qualities, her abilities, her disabilities, her numerous hospital admissions, all her different doctors, and about the special needs world Grace lived in, along with other severe multi-handicapped children. Mrs. Bowen explained how, in some ways, her Grace was actually quite lucky, comparatively speaking, because Grace had a pretty face, could walk with supervision, could talk to a certain degree, and didn't need a wheelchair; many of the profoundly disabled are often imprisoned in wheelchairs their whole lives, crippled unmercifully from birth, severely deformed in one form or fashion, and often cannot speak at all, although those that care for them can somehow decipher their wants, needs, and emotions from more subtle measures. The store clerk was genuinely fascinated and the conversation went on for several minutes. They were both lucky no one else was waiting in line.

Eventually, little Shannon nudged her mother and expressed the desire to get going as kids often do; and so they did.

꩜

On the car ride home, Shannon asked the question, "Mommy, what exactly is an angel?"

Mrs. Bowen was a little lost in reflection. She pondered the question and before answering, she looked into her rear-view mirror for a second to check for any traffic behind her and then peered ahead through the front windshield at the open road ahead. She made a quirky-type facial expression that exhibited her efforts of consideration and thought, and then she answered her daughter.

"I've always thought of an angel like in the movies, Shannon—either as a beautiful little cherub with wings, or a mighty warrior carrying a sword and shield, or a crafty wise old man hiding nearby in the shadows, whispering to a person about what to do in a difficult situation. Other than that, though, I'm not really sure. I do think, though, that angels are everywhere around us. Does that answer your question?"

Shannon smiled in a simple, childish, satisfied way. She answered, "Yes, Mommy, it does."

꩜

The Bible defines an angel as a messenger of God. It is a pure spirit created by God and employed by God as the minister of His will. Old Testament theology included the belief in angels as spiritual beings or intelligence of heavenly residence. The Bible mentions only three angels directly by name (Michael, Gabriel, and Raphael), yet, the concept of angels is referenced throughout the

Bible in numerous passages. The Lord Jesus Christ often spoke of angels as being in seven different classes or categories and with power bestowed on them directly by God. Some interpretations of the Bible and religious texts, set forth angels as simply existing in the world we live in by God's design for different virtues, qualities, and powers, such as wisdom, peace, harmony, faith, humility, love, charity, hope, miracles, grace, and compassion. Other interpretations present angels as guardians to guide and watch over people. Angels are often described as purely spiritual beings with intelligence and free will, whose name, in fact, indicates their mission as ministers of God and they can intercede for people. In many presentations about the existence of angels in our lives, we are simply asked to believe that they exist.

> *Every time a bell rings, it means that an angel got his wings.*
> – It's a Wonderful Life

∽∾

Mrs. Bowen and Shannon arrived home later that afternoon and quickly found Grace in the living room with her father. Grace was sitting happily on her father's lap, playing with long ribbons and strings in her hands. Together, Grace and her dad were watching a Philadelphia Phillies baseball game on TV. After Mr. Bowen gave his wife a detailed update on Grace's foods eaten for lunch, the medicine dosages received since mom had left, water amounts given so far that day, and the time of the last diaper change; they all sat together in the family room and watched the game together. While watching, Mrs. Bowen recanted for her husband the interesting exchange of earlier that day with the sales clerk at the angel store.

Shannon patiently waited for her mother to finish the recap and then directed a question at her father, "Daddy, is our Grace an actual angel?"

He sat there for a few minutes without saying a word. It was certainly a topic he'd thought about before. Eventually, he muted the TV and responded, "Shannon, I would answer that question this way. I would say, yes. I believe in my heart that severely disabled children like Grace are, in fact, angels on earth. I say that for three distinct reasons. First of all, because they have never sinned; they have never intentionally hurt anyone their entire lives. Their souls are completely pure." At this point Grace turned toward her father randomly as she often did and instinctively hugged him for no particular reason. She often had such poetic timing.

Mr. Bowen continued his explanation as he hugged Grace back, "The second reason, I say to people, Shannon, is because children like Grace suffer a tremendous amount on this earth. They suffer a lot like Jesus Christ did. They seem to suffer a great deal, almost as if they're suffering for the sins of others, certainly not for anything they ever did. It seems so totally unfair what children like Grace have to go through." Mrs. Bowen listened intensely. She loved to hear her husband's opinions on the subjects pertaining to their Grace; she sat on the family room couch nearby and smiled with the pride only a mother could have, and, particularly in this instance, the mother of a special needs child.

"The third reason, Shannon, I say, is because Grace loves people with total, unconditional love. She asks for nothing in return and she loves every single person she meets. I honestly couldn't imagine what more someone would think or want an angel to be. As we know, many of the caring people who work in the field of helping the disabled believe that children and adults like Grace will be the ones taking care of *us* in the next life."

With that thought-provoking detailed response hanging in the air, they sat together quietly and continued watching the Phillies baseball game, which was one of their favorite things to do together as a family.

Angels are speaking to all of us… Some of us are only listening better.
– Anonymous

GRACE

Here's the one with such a face
That all of us will seek for Grace,
So full of charm with virtue mild
This gift to us this graceful child.

You always know when Grace takes wing,
The sun will shine, the birds will sing;
And everywhere in every place
The world will seem so full of Grace.

By Grace of God we use our time
To contemplate these things divine;
And when we take our slumber here,
We have no doubt or even fear
That Grace of God will guide us on,
Protect our night from dusk to dawn,
And every morn her wish will be,
We'll rise anew so gracefully.

And when the day is nearly done,
With each success that you have won,
It's then God's angels sing with glee,
We're glad to grant our Grace to thee.

– John Wm. Sisson

Amazing Grace Margaret

The music therapist had his hands full of equipment as he made his way across the back lawn, headed toward the gazebo area to set up for the scheduled late-afternoon group session at the St. Michael's summer camp for kids. The daily summer camp program, known as Camp Sunrise, had over fifty children enrolled and offered the kinds of things one might expect at a typical summer camp for children, only this particular camp had a dedicated sensory focus for the disabled for numerous reasons, including the fact that most of the participants enrolled were in wheelchairs. The camp offered arts and crafts, indoor swimming, music, entertainment, nature explorations, field trips to fun locations in the Philadelphia area, picnics, daily prayer sessions in the chapel—and for those whose parents confirmed participation, small-tractor hayrides around the picturesque grounds of the facility as well as holiday theme parades.

One of the unique aspects about Camp Sunrise when compared to most other camps, and besides the severe, multi-handicapped nature of the children, was the incredibly dedicated and caring staff that worked there. The staff included nurses, care aides, feeding therapists, occupational therapists, speech therapists, the activities director, the food service department, social services personnel, the security team, van drivers, and an army of local, college age workers who came each summer and applied for the summer camp jobs. All the college age staff members proudly wore the official t-shirts each day, which read Camp Sunrise on the front and were all labeled on the back "Camp Counselor."

"Good afternoon, Mr. O'Mara," said the facility administrator, speaking to the music therapist as he arrived at the gazebo.

Mr. O'Mara put down his heavy black cases and instruments and answered, "Yes, good afternoon, Dolores. What time do you want me to start?" He looked around and added, "Where are all the children?" As he spoke, one of the many camp counselors was approaching Dolores in a fast walk, coming out from the main building and with apparent purpose. The young camp counselor looked to be about twenty years old with short brown hair. Dolores raised her one hand toward the counselor motioning for the young lady to hold her comments for just a moment.

Dolores turned back to Mr. O'Mara and said, "The children are all inside getting changed right now. They had a nature exploration adventure in the woods next to the playground after lunch and then they all went swimming in the indoor pool. They should be outside again in about ten minutes or so. Please, just take your time setting up. We'll start in a little bit. And, we're certainly glad to have you again this year." Mr. O'Mara then started to unpack his things and Dolores turned to speak now with the camp counselor.

"Yes, Colleen?" inquired Dolores politely. The energetic young camp counselor caught her breath and answered, "The girls' nurse asked me to tell you that Gracie had another minor seizure while they were changing her, but to tell you that she seems okay now. She came out of it pretty quickly. They are all watching her. They were putting ointment on the rash Grace sometimes gets because of all the diapers, when the seizure occurred. And Grace's mother is in there too, because, as you know, she's here helping for the day. But other than that development with Grace, everyone else should be outside in about five minutes."

The music therapist chimed in from a short distance away, "Excuse me. I'm sorry to overhear. But are you speaking about Grace, the curly blond-haired girl who was born on All Saints' Day and looks like an angel?" Dolores and Colleen both smiled and nodded.

"I remember her from last year," he went on. "I spent a lot of time with her playing nursery rhymes and religious songs. She's amazing. She really enjoys music and, as I recall, she had some fascinating abilities to remember the words. She is such a happy little girl, too. I hope she's okay. Also, isn't she the child who was picked out of crowd of thousands and blessed by Pope John Paul II?"

Dolores answered, "Yes, exactly, on all fronts, Mr. O'Mara. In fact, Colleen here is a friend of Grace's family. Colleen's oldest brother is good friends with Grace's dad." Colleen nodded her head once again to agree.

"Wonderful. I love small-world-type stuff," said Mr. O'Mara, as he meanwhile continued to unravel an electric cord.

Dolores smiled and continued. "Yes and I'll also tell you, Mr. O'Mara, something you'll be particularly glad to hear. We have significant extra money in our entertainment budget this summer because Colleen's brother and some other friends of Grace's parents have had a few fundraisers over the last year or so to raise money for our little summer camp program. There was a golf outing last fall, a big picnic fundraiser at the end of last summer, and Colleen's brother organized a retro 'Let's Relive Our Prom Night" party for all their family and friends. The net proceeds from all these events went to our St. Michael's Camp Sunrise budget. In addition, one of Grace's great aunts donates a significant amount of money to us each year, specifically designated for the summer camp program. Also, we have several foundations and big charitable donors now in our corner because of Grace. We are quite blessed. Our little Grace is a bit of a fundraising lightning rod."

Young Colleen quickly added in, "And she's very special to me personally, too. When I first met Grace last summer, I was a business major at my college. After spending last summer working with Grace and all the other wonderful children here, I changed my major to special education. Grace inspired me. I just love working with these special needs children. It's so rewarding. I feel lucky to work here." She waited a few seconds and then added, "Okay, excuse me. I have to get back to my group."

⚬⚬⚬

A short time later, the side doors of the St. Michael's Great Room opened and, in waves, all the children were brought outside. The group, mostly in wheelchairs, slowly assembled in a big half-circle on the lawn around the gazebo for the music therapy session. As the camp counselors and care aides pushed the children's wheelchairs, one could not help but notice both the severe crippling disabilities of the children, which was at first quite difficult to see, but also the caring interactions going on between the loving staff and the children. While the physical disabilities in view were the types often so hard for the general public to accept, the plight of these children of God also exuded such an innocent vulnerability that was quite endearing if one paid attention.

An intuitive observer would eventually conclude that while many of these children could not express themselves like normal, healthy children might, these children did, nonetheless, express themselves in their own particular ways. There was just a skill involved to comprehend and interpret, and the staff at Camp Sunrise clearly had learned the subtle noises, motions, and facial expressions that these special children made for their every day wants, needs, joys, and simple happiness.

At the back of the moving crowd, heading toward the gazebo area, was eight year-old Grace Margaret Bowen. She was walking awkwardly, but determined with her mother and the camp counselor, Colleen, at her sides… all of them together, holding hands. Grace was one of the few ambulatory children at the camp. Although considered legally blind, Grace could see a little and she walked with assistance and supervision; she had to wear a helmet for safety. The helmet resembled those used by children riding a bicycle.

As Grace's mother and Colleen placed Grace in a chair between them, encircled around the gazebo, one of the many nurses on the Camp Sunrise staff approached from behind, carrying several syringes full of medicine. The nurse had four large syringes with each medicine being a different color. The nurse spoke out as she approached. "Grace Margaret, it's time for some of your medicines." The look on Grace's face exhibited that she was processing the words she had heard to determine who had said them. Although she was severely mentally retarded (with the politically correct and preferred word being "special"), and despite the fact she could not add three plus two if given a simple math problem, Grace answered the nurse without even hesitating, turning, or looking.

"Miss Mary Jo," Grace answered back sweetly, demonstrating that she knew exactly who was talking to her from behind, which exhibited her rather unbelievable ability to know so many people by the mere sound of their voice. The total number of people in her mental memory bank, according to her parents, counted out to be the astounding number of approximately 100. Mary Jo, the nurse, then quickly sneaked in from behind and administered a few quick injections of medicine, one at a time, which Grace took orally in a way that resembled feeding a baby bird. While the medicine was being administered, Grace's mother and Colleen softly sang nursery rhymes to distract Grace and help with the overall process. They didn't want her to gag herself on purpose, which she often did because she hated taking all the medicine each and every day.

When finished with the medicine, nurse Mary Jo turned to Grace's mother and said, "I have to tell you…this morning, I sat with Grace and we prayed for ten minutes. She is absolutely unbelievable. She knows all the words to several different prayers by heart. She was even helping me along when I messed up. She knows the "Hail Mary," the "Our Father," and the "Glory Be." Grace's mother smiled, nodded, and put her hand lovingly up to her daughter's face. A few short moments later, the music therapist Mr. O'Mara began his afternoon performance. He started out with some classic nursery rhyme songs because he remembered what a big hit that had been the year before, especially when he and Grace had ended up doing a duet with one of the songs. He had been surprised to learn the year before that Grace somehow had the uncanny ability for music memorization with the lyrics, beats, and rhythms; with nursery rhymes being her preferred specialty because she had heard them repeatedly so much over her lifetime, sung to her by her family and caregivers. One of the doctors had explained to Grace's parents that one part of her otherwise abnormal, impaired brain, in fact, worked quite well for Grace and to a degree even better than for most normal, completely healthy people, which raised the ability in this area for Grace almost to the level of being a savant. The incredible irony being that she couldn't do *any* normal daily activities of life on her own without help from others, yet she had dozens of entire songs and religious prayers completely memorized.

The music therapist continued his performance as the afternoon sun warmed the children and the staff of Camp Sunrise. And, the faces of the children were happy.

∽

Question for the reader:

1.   Why is Grace amazing?

THE GALA

The emcee looked so elegant. She walked gracefully and with a quiet confidence over to the podium located in the front middle of the ballroom at the prestigious Overmink Country Club. She displayed a distinct sophistication as she stood with perfect posture and reviewed her notes. Occasionally, she would glance up to peruse the room and then smile. She seemed to be enjoying taking in the ambiance with the orchestra playing softly on the stage behind her and the bustling silent auction tables, which ran in rows over to her right. The busy silent auction tables had dozens of people milling about, all trying to outdo one another with the highest bid for the items. There was a unique crowd in attendance—all present for the legendary cocktail hour. The crowd consisted of dapperly dressed gentlemen drinking martinis and aged scotches and gorgeous ladies in beautiful gowns, sipping champagne in gold-rimmed fluted glasses. The ballroom itself sparkled with the festive "Roaring Twenties" theme decorations everywhere and from the huge Waterford crystal chandelier hanging in the center of the room. The mahogany wood trim and Old World Gatsbyesque décor invoked the atmosphere of an era gone by and was a setting much like a Newport, Rhode Island, mansion in the heyday.

The group in attendance for the special fundraising evening was a remarkable "Who's Who" list of some of the most successful, wealthy, and philanthropic of the Philadelphia Main Line, all gathered for the dual purposes of helping a good cause and a night out to have some great fun. After a few short moments of soaking in the exceptional surroundings, the emcee checked her watch and then tapped on the microphone to make sure it was working.

"Good evening, everyone," she started out. "Please, may I have your attention?" She raised her hands slightly as she spoke, to help with the calming of the boisterous crowd. Her soft, yet confident demeanor and her impeccable attire together, exuded the type of class many often strive for in life. And, her striking, God-given natural beauty certainly helped obtain everyone's attention. She came across as in the middle-age category, but appeared a good ten years younger than her birth certificate might offer. She had an unmistakable look that provided immediate wonderment to all who pondered as to what she must have looked like back in her youth. She looked like a "Miss America" probably looked like later in life. She had made it a point to meet everyone in the room when they arrived earlier that evening, so there was no need for any further introductions.

"Could I have everyone's attention for a few minutes?" she asked. As the noises of the crowd gradually simmered, the emcee glanced over at the huge picture-board propped on an easel to her left. The board was full of pictures of severely disabled, multi-handicapped children. The photographs depicted approximately forty children, with almost all of them being in wheelchairs. The children were dressed wearing different Halloween costumes. Many of the children, one could notice, suffered from crippling physical deformities, in one way or another, but together they seemed in the pictures to be happy and enjoying a fall-themed outside afternoon event.

The emcee resumed her presentation, "As everyone here knows, we gather each year for this annual gala to raise money for St. Michael's Home for Children, which is a facility in our Archdiocese that cares for severe, multi-handicapped, disabled children; the most fragile of God's children. Our auxiliary group, called 'The Wings of St. Michael's' has been in existence for over ninety-years now and each year at this event, we honor one of our members and give them the prestigious 'Golden Wings Award,' in thanks for their distinct efforts and financial support over the years for this great, great cause." She put on her reading glasses at that point and then continued.

"Now, for those who may be newer to our group, we also always like to pay tribute to the past winners and those distinguished names, you will see, are listed in the program books placed on the tables. So, please take the time to read the impressive list sometime tonight, perhaps while eating the delicious dinner. Now, in a few minutes, the silent auction and cocktail hour will be concluded and we will then all be seated for dinner. While we're eating, the orchestra will continue to play. Then, during the dessert, we will conduct the live auction portion of the program, which includes some truly unbelievable donated items this year, such as exquisite jewelry, week-long vacations at New Jersey shore houses, spa prizes for the ladies, Philadelphia sports team tickets, restaurant gift certificates, and several golf foursomes at some of the most prestigious country clubs in the area. So, get your checkbooks out and credit cards ready, ladies and gentlemen. Then, after the live auction is finished, we will have the presentation to this year's distinguished award winner. After that, we'll have more music, drinking, and dancing." She paused and took a sip of water from a glass on the podium table.

"But, before we all sit down for our dinner tonight, this year, we on the executive committee, thought we would do something a little different. We've asked one of the parents of a child involved in the St. Michael's programs to come here tonight and speak to you about the wonders of St. Michael's from their perspective as a parent and to, perhaps, help remind us of what our mission is all about." As she finished her sentence, I moved a few steps closer to her and prepared to walk to the podium.

The emcee paused again, and then said, "So, without further adieu, ladies and gentlemen, I would like to introduce, and this is how he asked me to introduce him, please welcome…Grace's dad."

∽∾∽

"Good evening, everyone," I offered, as I arrived at the podium and adjusted the microphone height. "It is certainly a distinct honor to be asked to speak to you tonight, especially about something as dear to the hearts of me and my family, and that is St. Michael's." As I spoke, I took out a sheet of paper from my suit coat jacket and placed it on top of the podium table. I formally introduced myself and then continued.

"Our oldest daughter Grace has been involved at St. Michael's for over twelve years now. We believe, like many others, that St. Michael's is the best facility of its kind in the entire country for what they do for multi-handicapped, disabled children, and everything they do is done with such love." As I spoke, I could tell I was a little nervous, so I raised my voice inflection to help keep it from cracking.

"Permit me to give you all a little perspective and insight tonight, which is something that these special needs children provide to us every single day… *if* we pay attention. I always say 'we can always benefit from a little perspective in life.' Our daughter Grace is now fifteen years old. She has been hospitalized forty-nine times in her lifetime so far. She has had multiple surgeries and some of the procedures would make you cry to hear about. She has fifteen different doctors that she sees on an annual basis for one reason or another, and she takes approximately seventeen doses of medicine each and every day. She suffers from random seizures, which can occur at any time and she cannot eat regular food unless it is pureed. In fact, she cannot do most of the normal activities that we take for granted and do each day to care for ourselves. She is also legally blind. She will never be able to live on her own. She has had numerous ER hospitalizations, resulting in so many IVs inserted into her veins over the years that her little wrists and ankles are severely scarred...." At that point, I became emotional and had to stop. I cleared my throat and tried to regroup.

I reached for a tissue out of my suit coat pocket and raised it to dab the corners of my eyes. I slowly endeavored to regain my composure and looked around the room as a means for a helpful pause. As I scanned the vast room, I noticed the faces of many in the crowd who were listening intensely and displaying genuine concern.

After clearing my throat again to help, I continued, "However, I must tell you folks that my wife and I consider ourselves lucky. I say that because our daughter Grace, despite all her medical problems and all her disabilities, is the happiest little girl we've ever seen and she absolutely flourishes in the St. Michael's program. All of the fundraising that you folks do for St. Michael's is incredible and it has resulted in so many facility improvements over the years, such as the outdoor flower memory walking garden, the big family entertainment room called the 'Great Room,' the special sensory room and, most recently, the magnificent new indoor swimming pool. All of these wonderful projects enable these special needs children of God to have some simple joys in their life and it adds so much to their quality of life overall." I felt a little shot of confidence at this point and again scanned the crowd.

"You see, ladies and gentlemen," I went on, "my wife and I, like many others, we believe that the St. Michael's children are God's angels on earth. These angels are God's gifts to all of us. And, in my opinion, it is *you* folks who enable these angels to fly and inspire people." I paused one more time and intentionally surveyed the room again, this time noticing that smiles were now starting to appear on many people's faces.

"Now, let me tell you one quite unique thing about our daughter Grace before we all sit down for a wonderful dinner. It is something I think you will find very interesting. Ten years ago, almost to the day, actually, we took our daughter Grace to Rome, Italy, along with a group from St. Michael's for the Millennium Jubilee Mass for the Disabled. We were part of big group from the Archdiocese. Handicapped people from all over the world went to Rome for this special jubilee Mass, which took place in the Basilica of St. Paul's Outside the Walls. The Mass itself was a true treasure for the 13,000 people there that day and a beautiful, long story for another time. However, at the Papal Audience event after the Mass, in a miracle of all miracles, our little Grace was picked out of a crowd of thousands and handed up to the Pope. That day she was hugged, kissed, and blessed by Pope John Paul II." I became visibly emotional again at this point and had to stop again. After several seconds, I continued.

"And as a result of that day, our Grace has become a bit famous around the Philadelphia area. She's known to many as the little girl who was friends with Pope John Paul II. She has been in various newspapers because of it, she's been on TV. We've been to *People Magazine*. In our simple estimation, she has been 'Blessed by a Saint.' So, I stand here before you tonight, humbly, as the parent of a little girl who we believe is a messenger of God and I want to thank you for all that you do to help her and all the other special needs children involved at St. Michael's. So, once again, thank you very much."

I stood there and garnered control of my emotions. Meanwhile, the entire ballroom erupted into a standing ovation. Many in the crowd were crying. After a few long poignant moments, the clapping slowly dissipating, I left the podium and walked over to join the emcee. And then…the party continued.

Question for the reader:

1. What does the word gala represent? Is it more than just an elaborate party?

LOOKING FOR GRACE

Little Shannon reached for a red and green sparkled sugar cookie, as she patiently waited for everything to get started. The big basket containing all the cookies and other treats was located in the center of each of the tables, surrounded by tiny milk cartons and juice boxes—all part of the holiday festivities for the annual Archdiocese of Philadelphia Christmas Party for Children. The event took place early each December at the big hotel in downtown Philadelphia. There were approximately 400 children altogether in attendance, all seated in the vast decorated ballroom, assembled around big, circular tables. The kids were of every ethnic background and came from all the different worlds involved with the Archdiocese's programs helping less fortunate children, and all under the proverbial umbrella of Catholic Social Services. The various programs and agencies represented at the event included: family service centers; community outreach programs to counter against violence and drugs; services for the mentally handicapped; adoption services; foster care programs; vocational programs; residential facilities for troubled teens due to criminal circumstances, parental neglect, or if coming from a severely dysfunctional family; and finally, emergency shelters for children. The programs benefited the children regardless of their creed, race, or color. Shannon Bowen, age nine and rarely one to be shy, crunched quietly on her cookie and waited. She was seated next to her older sister Grace, who was strapped in a special wheelchair-stroller combination and quietly played with a long white ribbon in her hands. Grace was ten years old and severely handicapped. Their mother sat on the far side of the stroller with an oversized carry bag full to the brim, prepared and ready to handle Grace's extensive everyday needs.

At this point, a news crew from one of the Philadelphia television stations walked in the back doors of the ballroom and a female reporter—famous for her popular weekly coverage of various entertaining and exciting happenings occurring around the Delaware Valley region—entered as the last contingent of the group. She immediately walked up to a member of the organizing staff for the event and politely asked, "Excuse me. Do you know where Grace Bowen is seated? Which table is the one for the children from St. Michael's?" The reporter seemed to receive a helpful answer to her inquiry and the news crew soon headed in the direction provided. It had been suggested to the reporter by her producer back at the station that she ask for Grace Bowen. The producer was a friend of Grace's father. The news crew then set up their cameras just off to the side of the two tables designated for the disabled children from St. Michael's.

The Christmas song *Santa Claus Is Coming to Town* started to play at exactly 2:30 sharp and Santa Claus himself jovially came exploding in the back left set of doors for the ballroom. Deafening roars from all the delighted children erupted throughout the room, which heightened the sheer excitement as jolly old Saint Nick waved and smiled. He looked around the vast ballroom and then headed straight for the St. Michael's tables, where he jostled the hair on the tops of a few of the children's heads as they sat in their wheelchairs. He quickly came upon, as if by obvious design, little Grace Bowen as the first child to receive a Christmas present from one of his big red gift bags. With the help of his loyal elves around him, Santa handed little Grace a beautifully wrapped present, which had her name on it, while he also leaned down and gave her a big hug. She returned the hug in a magnified fashion and she would not let go of him. As they hugged, he whispered in her ear and she seemed to listen intently. Little Grace had curly blond hair, red rosy cheeks, and porcelain white skin. She was both physically and mentally handicapped and legally blind; yet, she appeared content and extremely happy. Grace's slender, fawn-like arms wrapped around Santa's neck with a fierce determination; one couldn't help but notice and stare. The news camera crew soaked up the unique footage, which lasted for several, touching moments.

The footage with Santa was gold for the camera. There was a genuine loving connection visible, which carried right through the lens. Eventually, Santa gently concluded his embrace with little Grace and he gave her a big parting kiss on her cheek. He then stood up and continued upon his designated gift-giving route. He spent a good deal of time with the rest of the St. Michael's children, too, and then he worked the rest of the room, distributing both holiday cheer and the contents from his big red gift bags. The news crew followed him around the room, as he went from table to table.

Rumors often drifted at the event each year that Santa himself, as a young, hard-working teenager, had spent a few of his idle summers volunteering at the St. Michael's facility summer camp, helping with the care of the multi-handicapped disabled children there; and, thus, Santa had established an extra-special connection with them, which perhaps explained why he always started each year at the St. Michael's tables.

The Archdiocese's Christmas Party for Children each year provided a wonderful occasion for the children. The joy on their faces told the simple story. The event always began with the arrival of Santa and the distribution of the gifts. While Santa completed his mission around the room, a Philadelphia Archdiocesan high school band played Christmas songs on the stage in the front of the room. And, accompanying Santa in a festive parade of sorts around the room were costumed characters, cheerleaders, jugglers, and even a man walking on stilts—many of the volunteer entertainers were high school students from throughout the Archdiocese. After the parade ended, the then-sitting Cardinal or Archbishop of the Archdiocese would enter the room and speak to the children about the true meaning of Christmas. Following that presentation, there was a reenactment performance of the nativity scene on the stage. The actors for the nativity scene each year came from various arch-diocesan high school drama clubs. After the nativity play was concluded, the Cardinal or Archbishop proceeded from table to table himself and had photographs taken with the children from all the different programs. He, too, usually started with the tables for the children from St. Michael's, knowing full well that their frail health and complicated medical conditions often affected how long they could stay at the event. Most of the children from St. Michael's were in wheelchairs and many had strict medicine schedules to keep.

The photographs of the Cardinal with the St. Michael's children often ended up in the Philadelphia newspapers the following day, along with comments on how these disabled children personified God's love for all his children, as well as the true holiday spirit of Christmas. The event overall, was a wonderful example of all the good being done by the Archdiocese and Catholic Social Services for children in need.

The proud history of the Archdiocese Christmas Party for Children traced back more than fifty years to 1956 when Cardinal O'Hara (then an Arch-bishop) decided that the event would be a good way to honor representative groups from the various facilities, institutions, and programs served by

Catholic Social Services and, at the same time, present a face for the children aided through the charitable donations of the annual Catholic Charities Appeal. The event was organized and conducted each year by a small volunteer committee of dedicated lay board members, all committed to the cause. For those involved, it was a truly a labor of love.

After, the nativity play was finished, the Cardinal ventured with his contingent over to the St. Michael's table and had photographs taken with the children. He, too, received a big hug from Grace, which once again became the favorite picture of the Cardinal's personal photographer and likely to be used in the next edition of the Philadelphia Catholic newspaper, *The Catholic Standard and Times*.

⌇⌇

A few hours after the event, in the kitchen of a two-story colonial house in suburban Philadelphia and just as the clock on the wall struck six o'clock exactly; a small boy of about seven years old, sat and watched TV with his mother at the kitchen table. Together, they waited for the television news to start and, especially, the footage about the Philadelphia Archdiocese's Christmas Party event earlier that day. The little boy turned and asked his mother, "Who are we looking for again, Mommy?"

She answered him, "We're looking for your cousin, dear, your cousin Grace. She goes to the Christmas Party for Children downtown every year and, somehow, she usually ends up being on TV and in all the newspapers. So, we're looking for Grace."

⌇⌇

Question for the reader:

1.   Who is looking for Grace and why?

A Special Bedtime Prayer

Grace rested her head on the fluffy white pillow and her curly, blond hair framed around her face like soft golden silk. She closed her eyes and slowly, she started to drift off to sleep. As she did, her inner thoughts carried throughout the room like a leaf swirling on a clear and windy autumn day—dancing almost magically in the corner of a building. Grace kept her ocean-blue eyes closed as she internally said her evening bedtime prayers. She laid there peacefully still, with her white porcelain skin and rosy red cheeks. Being a sixteen-year-old girl with severe physical and mental disabilities, she generally prayed in her own particular way. The prayerful thoughts this night were as follows: *Dear Pope John Paul II, it's me, Grace. I don't know if you remember me, but we met once. It was back in the year 2000 at the Millennium Jubilee Mass for the Disabled, actually at the Audience afterward. I was six back then. I was the little girl in the red Christmas dress that you picked up, hugged, and blessed.*

I realize that you are in heaven now, probably helping God with a lot of important stuff. I'm sorry to bother you, but I'm praying to you because my dad asked me to. You see, one of my dad's close friends is sick with cancer. I don't know what cancer is exactly, but it sounds pretty terrible. My dad's friend Tim lives far away from us, down in a place called Florida; but my dad told me that they grew up together. My dad and I sit together and pray for his friend every Sunday. Anyway, I was wondering if you could see what you could do to help. Could you please talk to God and Jesus about it?

At the exact moment Grace finished those specific prayerful thoughts, she heard noises at the doorway entrance to her room. So, she stopped her prayers and listened. She figured, at first, that it was probably her mother opening the door to check on her or, perhaps, her sister was playing another one of her silly, childish games. Grace remained quiet and still, while she listened to try to determine the source of the noises.

Despite all her disabilities, Grace could hear quite well. Her communication skills and aptitude with sounds, songs, and lyrics actually defied logic. In fact, some of her teachers at the Main Line School for the Blind thought she may even be a savant of sorts, when it came to music, people's voices, and noise associations. Although she was severely handicapped and couldn't add three plus two if asked a simple math problem, she knew more than 100 different people by the mere sound of their voice alone, and she'd completely memorized numerous songs and prayers, all of which was quite hard for many experts to explain.

In time, the noises in the room sounded more and more like a breeze of air flowing through an open window, and then someone folding clothing while pulling on a drawer at the same time. The particular noises led Grace to the possible conclusion that it might be her mother putting away clean laundry or updating Grace's ever-changing adolescent wardrobe. Her mother constantly worked with Grace, regarding her clothes—trying on new shirts, dresses, and pants, and evaluating different outfits. Her mother always wanted Grace to look nice. But, as the noises continued, Grace could tell it was not her mother in the room, at all. The noises repeated every ten seconds or so, and now seemed to also include a faint, cord-like strumming, as if an instrument was being played far off in the distance. Grace thought, perhaps, one of the neighbors, down the street, was having a party. Some of their neighbors were always having parties.

She then considered again that maybe her younger sister, Shannon, aka "Sissy," was responsible for the noises. Grace surmised Sissy was probably sitting in her own room across the hallway, listening to music, either on her expensive new laptop computer or on her iPod. Grace had no use for such modern, technological devices, but her fifteen-year–old younger sister could not be separated from them. Their parents had imposed regulated hours during the school week for Sissy and her technology items, but since it was a Friday night, that could explain the noises. After a few more minutes, though, Grace remembered that Sissy had gone out earlier for the evening with friends and probably wasn't home, yet. Sissy had gone to a high school dance at the local boy's prep school.

Grace hoped her sister was having fun at the dance and, at the same time, wondered what it must be like to go to one of them. It wasn't the type of social event Grace customarily attended. She did fun stuff, though, just different.

Since Grace could walk a little, she actually had a big advantage over some of her closest friends, who were all restricted to wheelchairs. Grace loved to repeat her friend's names over and over again. There was Nay Nay, Nicky, Bengale, Brittany, Jake, April, Jia, Cholie, and Destiny, to name a few. Grace had a lot of friends. And, Grace certainly loved to dance, too. She always danced when they had birthday parties at school. Grace especially loved it when it was her own birthday because, in addition to a party at school, she would always get to go to Mass, since her birthday was on All Saints' Day. Grace truly loved going to Mass.

Grace knew that whenever she did get to go on a special school trip with her classmates somewhere, though, she had to always have either her mother or a nurse with her because of possible seizures, which could happen suddenly and without warning. When Grace had a seizure, it was a big ordeal. She needed a quick injection of medicine to try and bring her out of it and also she would receive oxygen from the portable oxygen tank, always with her when she traveled—all because of the time she had stopped breathing completely as the result of a nasty, long seizure. After the seizures finally did stop, she usually ended up going to the hospital in order for the doctors to figure out the cause; a list which included a shunt infection, a shunt malfunction, a bowel obstruction, urinary tract infection, pneumonia, more kidney problems, her medication levels were off, the flu, or a virus of some kind. And, sometimes…there wasn't any reason at all for the seizures.

Grace decided to change her own topic of thought and she reached all around on her blanket, trying to find the long pink ribbon she had been playing with in her hands—she loved playing with ribbons and strings—but, instead, she touched one of the guard rails affixed on the sides of her bed, which were there for her safety. Just touching the high metal safety rails reminded Grace of all those times she'd been admitted to the hospital.

Her father recently had said to someone that the current up-to-date total was now fifty admissions over her lifetime so far. She had been through so many tough medical illnesses. Her father often told her she was like the old cartoon character "Gumby," who was known for being incredibly resilient, only she was much, much prettier. When Grace stayed overnight in the hospital, her dad would always sleep in the room with her at night to make sure she didn't fall out of the hospital bed or try to get up and walk out. He, generally, slept right next to her on one of those vinyl hospital chairs that extend out into a small cot. It didn't look very comfortable. Since Grace was profoundly mentally retarded and blind, but could walk, the doctors considered that a pretty dangerous combination. She couldn't be left alone for a minute in the hospital. And, she had admittedly tried to escape the hospital on more than one occasion. No one likes being in the hospital. With that in mind, Grace now wondered if her father had snuck into her room and was now lying on the floor next to her bed until she fell asleep. He did that sometimes. Maybe that explained the noises.

Grace yawned, rubbed her eyes, and then resumed her nighttime prayers. *Well, Pope, I'm getting pretty tired now and I'm going to go to sleep. Please do what you can for my dad's friend. Thank you. Amen.*

As Grace finally drifted off to sleep, her bedroom door gently closed.

TALKING WITH GRACE

Q: "How are you today, Grace?"
A: "Good."
Q: "How was school this week?"
A: "Good."
Q: "Grace, lets say a nursery rhyme together. Twinkle, twinkle…"
A: "Little star."
Q: "How I wonder…"
A: "What you are."
Q: "Up above the world so high…"
A: "Like a diamond in the sky."
Q: "Okay, Grace. Let's pray together. Hail Mary…"
A: "Full of Grace."
Q: "Our Father…"
A: "Who art in heaven."
Q: "Grace, what is the story with Aunt Gertrude?"
A: "She's a pain in the neck."
Q: "And Grace, what is the story with your Gamma?"
A: "Sweetie Pie."
Q: "Grace, what do you always tell Gamma? To be…"
A: "Be careful!"
Q: "Grace, how much is three plus two?"
A: "Take a walk. Picnic. Ribbons. Sissy."
Q: "Grace, who is your friend in Rome?"
A: "The Pope."

Q: "Who is your favorite rock group?"
A: "U2."
Q: "Grace, let's count together. One…"
A: "Two."
Q: "Three…"
A: "Four."
Q: "Nineteen…"
A: "Twenty."
Q: "Let's count together in French. Une…"
A: "Duex."
Q: "Trois…"
A: "Quatre."
Q: "Grace, what time is it?"
A: "Ribbons. Take a walk. Chicken nuggets."
Q: "Grace, who is one of your friends and classmates?"
A: "Nay Nay."
Q: "Who else?"
A: "Jake."
Q: "Who else?"
A: "Bengelese."
Q: "Grace, what is your bus driver's name?"
A: "Mr. Herrrrman."
Q: "Grace, do you like to take medicine?"
A: "No."
Q: "Grace, what do you want to do today?"
A: "Picnic. Go to the movies. Bowling. Take a walk."
Q: "Grace, our parish priest said to say 'Hello' to you. His name is Father…"
A: "McEvit."
Q: "Grace, how old are you?"
A: "Seventeen."
Q: "Grace, who loves us?"
A: "Jesus."

Quotes and Comments about Grace

1. Doreen Bowen (Grace's Mother) – "Grace is our angel; she is pureness and happiness personified. Grace is a gift from heaven. It is truly an honor to be her mother."

2. Margaret Obal (Grace's Grandmother) – "The first time I held my beautiful granddaughter was in the delivery room after her traumatic birth and I knew then, there was something unique and special about her. Over the years, I have watched in awe her courage, her determination, her abilities, and how she inspires people. She is truly 'Amazing Grace'."

3. Joanne Gill (Friend and Home Health Aide for Grace as an Infant) – "The first time I met Grace, she melted my heart. I believed then and I believe now, that she is an angel from God put here on earth to touch as many people as she can. Anyone who meets Grace never forgets her. I donated blood for one of Grace's surgeries and it was an honor. I am a better person for being part of Grace's life."

4. Doug Dunn (Friend, Former Employee at CSS residential care facility for medically fragile, multi-handicapped children and Occasional Wearer of a Santa Claus Costume at Parties for Children) – "I go to spend time with Grace when I need help dealing with tough things that are going on in my life. I go for what I call 'Gracie time'."

5. Katie Meehan Ciolko (Friend of Grace's Parents) – "When you hug Grace, *you* feel better."

6.   Reverend Joseph J. McLaughlin (Pastor of St. Vincent de Paul Parish in Richboro, PA) – "Our parish patron, St. Vincent de Paul, said, 'We are commissioned not only to love God, but to cause Him to be loved.' I see Grace accomplishing that by her love, her innocence, and her beauty. You come to love Grace, not because of what she does, but because of who she is—and that is the kind of love that we are called to have for God. I believe Grace exemplifies and inspires that kind of love."

7.   Beth Fisher Folino (Friend and Nurse for Grace) – "To me, Grace is an inspiration, an achiever, someone who loves unconditionally. She gives the best hugs—the kind that come from the heart. My world would not be the same without 'Grace' in my life. Perhaps, the best way for me to explain how I feel about Grace is to tell you that she was in my wedding party."

8.   Jackie Cahill (Friend and Nurse for Grace) – "When I think back to the day that Grace was selected out of the crowd at random to be hugged and blessed by the Pope, I am always struck with this feeling of humbling gratitude for being present in that auditorium. To see someone you know, someone you've cared for, someone whose cross to bear in life is much heavier than your own, be lifted by the Pope and blessed, was for me, awe-inspiring. I will never forget the feeling of that moment. I was fortunate to be holding a video camera and I somehow managed to capture the events on film, despite shaky hands and teary eyes. The Pope seemed to look at Grace and instantly see the beautiful, perfect soul that she is. I believe that all of us who were with her that day were indeed blessed that day by association with her. I will also never forget the look on Grace's father's face as he carried Grace back to her seat after she was blessed. His face was a combination of humility, raw emotion and sheer joy. I have heard Grace's parents say since 'that was the biggest day of Grace's life' and I am so grateful for the experience."

9.   Mary Connors (Friend and Nurse for Grace) – "When you are with Grace, you know you are with a very special child. Grace somehow never forgets your name and she always gives you a hug. I think Grace is the light in a sometimes dark world. Life can be a difficult journey and it's not always easy to know which way to go; however, when you are with Grace, you live in the moment and appreciate what God has given you today."

10.   Rosemary Wachinski (Grace's Great Aunt) – "Grace is a sweet, beautiful, joyful, angelic child. I believe she was sent by God to special parents to offer

comfort and encouragement to those in need. She came into my life when I needed both. She truly is a blessing from above. I feel honored that her parents share her with me and the world."

11. Susan Carney Smuck (Friend of Grace's Parents) – "Being around Grace is like a refreshing breeze. She is nurturing in a spiritual way and she makes me feel good about myself, despite any imperfections. Grace accepts everyone for who they are without reservation. She has a karma and loving glow about her that is like a healing stream. Grace loves everyone."

12. BJ Flynn (Friend, Nurse, and Former Employee at CSS residential care facility for medically fragile, multi-handicapped children) – "The epitome of God's love is captured all in the being of Grace. She is innocent with a great sense of humor, loving, and she has incredible determination. Grace has been a gift from the Almighty; He chooses to radiate His love through her. I am blessed to have her in my life."

13. Pam Samuels, M.Ed. (Friend and Program Director at CSS residential care facility for medically fragile, multi-handicapped children) – "As someone who works every day with children who have severe disabilities, I am amazed at Grace's ability to imitate words and spoken patterns. And, I am fascinated how she learns to identify a person by their voice after meeting them only once. Given her medical conditions and severe disabilities, her abilities defy explanation. I love talking to Grace and taking walks with her. Grace is my friend and I consider her one of 'my children.' She is truly an angel."

14. Denise Clofine (Friend and the Administrator at CSS residential care facility for medically fragile, multi-handicapped children) – "Grace, despite the many challenges she faces each day, has the wonderful ability to teach us what is truly important in life. She is a little girl sent by God to remind us all about the simple priorities life should hold."

15. Donna Clayburne (Friend and Grace's Current One-on-One School Aide at preeminent Philadelphia area school for the blind) – "When I was initially asked many years ago to be Grace's one-on-one aide for school , I was overwhelmed with the complexity of Grace's care and, yet, at the same time, extremely excited to be part of Grace's life. I truly love Grace as if she were my own child. She is absolutely precious."

16. Ann Kneafsey (Friend and Employee at CSS residential care facility for medically fragile, multi-handicapped children) – "When I first saw Grace, she looked like a little cherub with her blue eyes and blonde curly hair. I was in awe. Over the years, my children and I would take walks with Grace and go to Mass with her. Spending time with her is enriching to your soul and she is a wonder to watch."

17. Grazielli Politano (Friend and Former Volunteer at CSS residential care facility for medically fragile, multi-handicapped children) – "I first met Grace in 2004 when I came to the United States from Brazil for college and I started to volunteer. I wanted to give love to those less fortunate than I. After I met Grace, however, this course was reversed. I was suddenly the one receiving *her* love. She is a superior soul who teaches us what's really important about life and she does it in a joyful way. No matter how long between my visits, when I'm with her and speak out her name, she replies back saying my name. I feel honored to be a part of Grace's life. I believe she is an angel from God who came into this world to lead our hearts to love."

18. John Mischler (Friend of Grace's Dad) – "They say God gives us grace to help us do what we need to do in life. I believe God gave us Grace Bowen to inspire us all to be the best we can be. I am one of many who can say my life has been touched by the gift of Grace."

19. Frank Boclair (Friend of Grace's Dad) – "My family deals every day with the challenges of a parent and young child, both fighting the same life-threatening disease. We face countless medical events that test our strength and resolve. I have learned that life is sometimes just very hard. Often, during our difficult moments, we reflect on the perseverance of 'Amazing' Grace Bowen, given all her disabilities and medical issues, as well as the tireless love, support, and positive outlook of her parents and her sister. We are inspired to move forward without complaining and to do so as a loving family unit."

20. Austin Meehan (Friend of Grace's Dad) – "As a long-time friend of Grace's dad, I am aware of all they have gone through with Grace's disabilities and her health problems. Somehow, I think it is Grace who gives her parents and her sister the strength to deal with all the adversity they have faced. She is like a keel of the ship."

21. Tom Vesey (Friend of Grace's Dad) – "Grace epitomizes how to handle adversity in life. Good captains were not made on a calm sea."

22. Dorothy Johnson (Friend and DCP/Aide at CSS residential care facility for medically fragile, multi-handicapped children) – "I first met Grace when she was three years old and she came to us because of her everyday care being so overwhelming. When I first laid eyes on her, I was mesmerized. I thought how she looked like an angel straight from heaven—she had such curly blond hair, pretty blue eyes, and fair skin. I have watched her grow from a little baby with so many medical problems to the beautiful young lady she is today. I have also seen how she has gone through so many illnesses, surgeries, and complications. I was there that day in Rome when Pope John Paul II took her into his arms and blessed her, and I have witnessed her incredible progress and her amazing abilities ever since that day. To me, she is a miracle."

23. Shannon Bowen (Grace's Sister) – "A spiritual energy comes from Grace. It's hard to explain, but you feel it when you are with her."

24. John Obal (Grace's Uncle and Godfather) – "Grace has an angelic charm and an infectious laugh that brings joy to those who know her."

25. Tom Wissert (Friend and Social Services Director at CSS residential care facility for medically fragile, multi-handicapped children) – "Grace touches others in a profound manner; they are forever changed in the moment of a warm smile or a simple 'Hello,' which often leads to reflection about the true meaning of life and what it really means to love."

26. Julia Vivanco (Friend, Occupational Therapist, and Program Coordinator at CSS residential care facility for medically fragile, multi-handicapped children) – "Coordinating events for special needs children like Grace is my passion. I remember sitting with Grace at the Broadway version of the *Lion King* and seeing her light up with her love of the music. She was clapping and singing throughout the entire show. She was so happy. I believe Grace is an angel and I consider it precious that she says 'Hi' to me every day."

27. Joan Vivanco (Julia's Mom, Friend, and Volunteer Extraordinaire at CSS residential care facility for medically fragile, multi-handicapped children) – "Grace is a special gift from God. Her pureness and simplicity is an example

for all of us. Maybe we should all play with ribbons and strings so we can be more like Grace."

28. Scott (Friend, Artist, and Employee at CSS residential care facility for medically fragile, multi-handicapped children) – "Grace is sweetness, love, and fun."

29. Greg McDermott (Friend of Grace's Mom and Dad) – "Grace brings pure joy to those privileged to be in her life. I always feel a positive influence when my family spends time with her, which lasts long after she sweetly whispers, 'Bye, Bye.'"

30. Dan Hogan (Friend of Grace's Dad) – "I have come to realize that Grace is, above all else, a gift from God, a blessing bestowed upon all that have known her. I have had the opportunity to introduce my family to Grace over the years and I am grateful for those encounters. When you spend time with Grace you gain perspective and receive insight about life, which helps you appreciate all you have."

31. Marie Berger (Friend and Nurse) – "Using a quote from Ann Frank – 'A clear conscience gives you peace.' – Grace gives us all peace."

32. Mary Adamow (Friend of Grace's Parents) – "Grace personifies all that is pure, good, and holy. Spending time with Grace has allowed me to experience a beautiful and precious gift. She has allowed me to say that I have been privileged to be close to one, who as her name implies, 'has truly found favor with God'."

33. Gloria Kanreck (Grace's Great Aunt) – "I have often been asked to ride along in the car when one of her parents is traveling with Grace in case she has a seizure. I am glad to be able to help out and I truly love just watching Grace. There is a simple harmony and beauty about the way Grace sits peacefully and listens to music, sings her favorite songs, and plays with her ribbons or strings in her hands. She is mesmerizing."

34. Lauren Saunders (Friend and Summer Camp Counselor at CSS residential care facility for medically fragile, multi-handicapped children) – "As a college student, I found myself searching for direction. I had not yet felt a passion for what I was meant to do with my life and the uncertainty caused me a great deal of distress. Then, in the summer before my senior year, I had my 'aha'

moment, which changed me forever. That was when I met Grace. When she reached to hold my hand on my first day as a summer camp counselor, I was put at ease and made welcome. Sitting with her, I felt love, inspiration, and direction all at the same time. I knew right then I wanted to work with special needs children for my career. That summer was one of the greatest experiences of my life. I feel that I am truly blessed to have met Grace. She has made me a better person, for which I will be forever grateful."

35. John Altimari (Friend of Grace's Parents and Neighbor) – "My family and I believe that Grace is a special girl who has angels all around her as she goes through life. We feel lucky to know her."

36. Dan Kelley (Friend of Grace's Dad) – "In 1997, my father donated a large sum of money to the Archdiocese of Philadelphia. He didn't want to specify where to allocate the money; his only request being that the funds be used for those that needed it the most. He eventually found out the entire donation went to a CSS residential care facility for medically fragile, multi-handicapped children which was where Grace was living. When he learned of the connection with Grace at the time, he was moved because he knew Grace was the child of my high school friend, Gerry Bowen. Then, approximately three years later, my father was in the hospital because of a severe stroke and other serious medical conditions. We in the family knew his days were numbered. During this difficult time, my friend Gerry called and asked to see me. Gerry told me he had something to give to my dad. I was unaware that Gerry and his family had just returned from a Pilgrimage to Rome. Upon meeting with Gerry, he presented me with a set of the rosary beads that Grace had been wearing when she was blessed by Pope John Paul II. I was blown away by this loving and most spiritual gesture. I visited with my father later that day at the hospital. My father was a proud Irish catholic and steadfast in his faith. I explained to him the story of Grace's journey to meet with Pope John Paul II and I placed the rosary beads in his hands. I was unsure whether or not he was fully grasping the details because of his deteriorating health. Suddenly, my father looked at me and mouthed the words, 'Thank Grace for me,' and then he started to cry. It was a divine moment and a cherished memory for me and my family. At his request, my father was buried with those rosary beads in his hands. My father never met Grace in person, but he had been touched by her presence."

37. Steve McKenna (Friend of Grace's Parents) – "My wife, Laurie, and I lived next door to the Bowens years back when Grace was born. Trying to offer comfort, we gave Gerry and Doreen a book titled: *When Bad Things Happen to Good People.* Looking back now, we say to ourselves, 'How wrong could we have been?' We wish, instead, we had told them that wonderful things happen to wonderful people, but sometimes just in mysterious ways. Maybe, that's what this book is all about. I hope so. Anyway, may God continue to bless the Bowen family with all His wonders."

38. Tom Rodman (Friend of Grace's Dad) – "I believe God has given Grace to the world for a reason. She has touched the lives of so many people already and, hopefully, many more will be touched with this book. Grace has been a true inspiration to many aspects of my family's life and she helps us be thankful each and every day."

39. Marilyn Maurer (Friend of Grace's Parents) – "I have worked for Grace's dad ever since she was born. I have heard him tell the stories of her heartbreaking medical trials and tribulations, as well as the heartwarming accounts of her wonderful interactions with others. I see Grace as an inspiring child who helps us appreciate the value of life and family and also prompts us to try and be the best person we can be with the time God has given us on this earth."

40. Debbie Saunders (Friend of Grace's Parents) – "My connection to Grace is twofold. I am a friend of the family by virtue of working for Grace's dad for many years and my youngest child Lauren worked as a camp counselor for several summers where Grace resides. I have learned to understand how Grace affects people in powerful ways. I know she had a great influence on my daughter for her life and her career, and I have witnessed on a daily basis how she works through her father to spread inspiration to people who need it. Personally, when I have had the opportunity to 'hang out with Grace' I have noticed how she helps renew your faith. She is fun and friendly to everyone she meets. Her charm and ability to exude unconditional love, given all her disabilities, is an amazing combination."

41. Christie Chicoine (Friend and Catholic Journalist) – "I have been privileged to write several newspaper articles about Grace over the years for the former Philadelphia Catholic newspaper, *The Catholic Standard and Times* and I have witnessed her charm and beauty in action. Despite all her medical

problems and disabilities, she brings about calm and love amid mankind's chaos. I love to give Grace ribbons and strings because I know they are her signature playthings and I also find the symbolism fascinating. Grace is gentle, sweet and full of glee."

42. Gene Wolstenhome (Friend of Grace's Parents and Involved with the Publishing of This book) – "Grace and her parents are inspirations to all of us."

43. Sister Martha Scheessele (Friend, Nurse, Divine Providence Nun, and Former Administrator at CSS residential care facility for medically fragile, multi-handicapped children) – When she first saw Grace, Sister Martha said, "We have in our midst, one of God's true angels."

44. Matthew Wachinski (Grace's Dad's Cousin) – "Years ago, when I learned the news of my cousin Gerry's daughter Grace having all the disabilities and medical problems, I thought how heartbreaking it must be not being able to see your child interact with the world as most of us do and to be burdened with such health and medical challenges. As an example, I believe the latest count of Grace's lifetime hospitalizations is approaching fifty. For me, that figure alone provides enormous perspective—knowing how stressful it can be taking a routine trip to the hospital to get one of my children a few minor stitches. Yet, when I speak with Gerry about Grace and about life, in general, the conversation always has an uplifting and positive tone. Perhaps, ironically, his source of strength and inspiration *is* his daughter Grace. Gerry has explained to me on multiple occasions that while Grace lacks certain abilities that we all take for granted, she has an angelic inspirational quality that fills all those around her with joy and happiness and she never complains. And, when I got to know Grace, I understood. Now, I figure that life for everyone has both sadness and joys, but you choose on what to focus and which path to walk. For Gerry and his wife, Doreen, they choose a path of optimism, motivation, and inspiration, despite life's problems. So from Grace and from my cousin, I have learned to choose the positive path, on which we are all welcome to travel. I now see Grace as a beacon for life—showing me how to live."

45. Colleen Dougherty (Friend and Social Services Representative at CSS residential care facility for medically fragile, multi-handicapped children) – "I met Grace seven years ago and she stopped me in my tracks. I felt humbled. The instant I met her, I felt a calmness, patience, and a warmness; nothing else

seemed to matter. I sat with her and listened to every word she offered with amazement. I felt like I was receiving grace from her. Grace has this effect on those that are open to the message."

46. Melanie B. Taylor (Friend and Grace's Former One-on-One School Aide at a preeminent Philadelphia area school for the blind) – "When I think about Grace's name, it is so perfect for her. She and I spent a lot of time together and I cherish my memories. I will always love her. Grace melts my heart."